I ANIMAL

KEVIN DEL PRINCIPE

To Katie &
The Bookly Club

Always be an animal!

K. D. Del P

Tumbleweed Books

Tumble through the pages of our books

I ANIMAL
Kevin Del Principe

Tumbleweed Books
Tumble through the pages of our books

HTTP://TUMBLEWEEDBOOKS.CA
An imprint of DAOwen Publications

I Animal / Kevin Del Principe

This is a work of fiction. Names, characters, places, and incidents either are the product of the author's imagination or are used fictitiously, and any resemblance to actual persons, living or dead, businesses, companies, events, or locales is entirely coincidental.

Cover art by Melissa Gebhardt

ISBN 978-1-928094-43-2
EISBN 978-1-928094-44-9

10 9 8 7 6 5 4 3 2 1

For Nikki and all the wild people/animals in our territory

ONE
THE FAT TRUTH ABOUT PEOPLE AND PLANES

There are plenty of ways to die.

I look over at the guy next to me. He's fat. Super fat. American-Elephant tourist fat. He has a wheelbarrow of a stomach sticking over where, I can only assume, his seatbelt is about to burst. When that happens, I'll be the first one taking cover because I plan on doing my best not to be shot dead by a fat man's seat buckle on a plane ride home.

Now, I don't judge. Not on fatness alone. The word fat may be indelicate, but it's important to be honest. Being truthful is all we really have in this wonderfully, terrible, totally meaningless, absolutely meaningful existence. The problem with honesty is that it's tied tightly to perception. Do not trust my perception. Believe me, it will let us down.

I think I'm becoming an animal. More on this later.

Fatty's eating the largest ham sandwich I've ever seen. The meat is packed so tight it's near explosion, much like Fatty himself. Fatty has one plastic coke bottle opened and the other in reserve. To his credit, Fatty's come prepared. One might imagine this level of preparation has all manner of utility if appropriated to more socially beneficial endeavors.

Unlike Fatty, I never eat on planes on account of the regrettable fact I have a weak stomach. A piece of Fatty's fatty ham breaks loose and dive-bombs onto the airplane tray right next to his two cokes. Ham-fisted, he picks up the pork, jams it into his gaping mouth, and in one surprisingly deft movement, sweeps mustard dribbling down the side of his mouth back inside his face-cave.

The Skinny Guy in front of Fatty flicks on a light so he can read a gossip rag featuring none other than the avant-garde poetess, Miley Cyrus. The motley lot of us, Fatty, Skinny, Miley, and I, are on a redeye out of Los Angeles. In case you're wondering, I'm not fat or skinny, just average, including that in the execution of my vocation. In fact, execution is probably the nearest word to describe my screenwriting career right now. My problem is I'm movie-making mediocrity trapped in a vessel that thinks it's divine. Either that, or I'm fucking awesome and the world's operating under a different set of awesomeness criteria.

I need to get home to Buffalo, fast. That's what you do when your mother is dying. You may have been son of the year, or a colossal blundering disappointment. Out of a sense of duty, if nothing else, you get your ass home. But this flight, of course, is not direct because I'm one of only several hapless assholes in the world who'd ever need to go to Buffalo from Los Angeles. You can get a flight from Las Vegas to Buffalo pretty easily. Buffalonians love to gamble. Buffalonians take a fuck-it attitude to their gambling. They figure they have little to lose when gambling because, fuck it, they're from Buffalo. It may be desperate thinking but at least Buffalonians feel their desperation.

People in Los Angeles are the most desperate people I know but they suppress it by doing cool activities. For instance, in LA, you're okay if you're a soul-eating corporate attorney as long as you also take jazz guitar lessons.

Due to some dastardly corporate airline reason, I couldn't get a connection out of Vegas to fly back with the gambling crowd. Instead, my connector is at CVG and I have a three-hour layover. For those unfamiliar, CVG is in Northern Kentucky, just outside Cincinnati – a beautiful metropolitan city if this is the post-apocalypse.

The overhead light flickers and the gossip rag's shadow is cast on the Skinny Guy's pale shroud. It's all rather Platonic and I'm reminded that all we can really see of each other in this wonderful absurdity of life are shadows of shadows ad infinitum. By this Skinny Guy's watch, I can tell he's got a few more *E pluribus unums* than me. I don't judge. Not on wealth alone.

Skinny Guy sips some pineapple juice. He finishes his read about Miley Cyrus and puts the magazine in the seat pocket in front of him. A smile creeps over my face as I imagine Skinny Guy leaving the magazine behind and then a weight lifter covertly picking it up on the next flight. Furthermore, I imagine the seat is actually a momma kangaroo and the pocket is her pouch, and inside her pouch is a vortex to another world where the only food is pineapples that demand to be called Miley. This is the sort of overactive imagination that has led to my lack of professional success as a screenwriter, and likely my failure at intimate relationships.

You can't be a screenwriter with an imagination. Producers prefer ugly, myopic screenwriters who can't write well. That way the producers feel better about their own poor looks and general lack of vision. I've also found women don't like imagination too much, though they often claim the contrary. Most women prefer men who see the world as a harsh reality they intend to fuck; not idealistic men who write alternative visions of potential worlds that might actually be a cool place to live. Why? Because change is scary.

Skinny Guy shuts off his overhead light. He presses the button on his seat and leans back to take a nap. Except, in doing so, Fatty's tray slams right into his gut.

Fatty quickly steadies his cokes as he sticks his head in the aisle toward Skinny. "Excuse me, sir. You're gonna have to move up!"

"What?" Skinny Guy squeaks.

Fatty points to his gut as if to say behold, look at what you have done. "You have to sit up!"

"I'm trying to sleep. Put up your tray," Skinny Guy responds.

Fatty freaks out like a caged animal out in the heat who reaches his limit when a child throws a dart at his ass and strikes home. He shakes the seat in front of him. Sweat pours down his face. Fatty looks to me pleadingly for help. I see his suffering so clearly, it's as if I'm a synecdoche and I can taste it. Ham with spicy brown mustard is the flavor. Like a coward, I avert my eyes. A stewardess jaunts up the aisle toward the melee. A brave soul must've had the courage to page her. The stewardess bends her head and speaks to Skinny Guy in a voice that commands attention, "Please sir, raise your seat."

"I paid good money for this seat and I want to lay down. And if I want to lay down I should be able to lay down," Skinny Guy retorts.

A fair argument, but admittedly I'm a huge fan of circular reasoning. I left Catholicism twenty years ago but if a new circular reasoning cult springs up in Venice, California where I live, I'll join in a heartbeat. The cult center will need to be in walking distance, however, because I refuse to get in my car when I'm home for the evening. Also, I'm not comfortable with mandatory cult meetings out of concern for my beach time. Most importantly, all the members need to be super-hot women who are easy for me to screw yet not too promiscuous with everybody else. They can blow each other now and again without my involvement, but that's it. If a circular reasoning cult pops up within these parameters, I will certainly become a member.

The stewardess re-articulates her position to Skinny Guy with the same detached, ice queen quality that ten years earlier I would have married and raised cold little urchins with in happy misery. It's a funny thing, my mother, Camilla, is anything but a distant woman. I suppose that was the point in going the opposite direction with my ex-wife, God rest her soul (she's not dead). My mother, God rest her soul, loved through suffocation. And I know what you're thinking... your mom's not dead yet either, and you're absolutely right. But there is the inevitability of death that is impossible to ignore when the woman who created you says she's only months from the very end because her big heart is failing.

Skinny Guy gives up all hope, much like I did in my marriage, and moves up his seat. Then the stewardess directs her attention to Fatty, "Put up your tray please, sir."

"How am I gonna eat?" Fatty spit-sprays.

For fuck's sake. The stewardess pulls out a trash bag and icily stares at Fatty, now free from his seat-cage, until he eats his last bit of ham sandwich and tosses his wrapper in her open trash bag and puts up his tray. He gulps his last coke, belches, and hands the bottle to the stewardess. She departs with the bottle like a trophy. For a second, she raises it in the air like she wants God or someone to acknowledge her cold existence.

Then, Skinny Guy suddenly tosses his Miley Cyrus rag in the trash. That's right, we're a bunch of celebrity-addicted zombies: dead but not; beautiful but not, flying across our pollution-filled American skies because we matter totally but don't utterly. We are the powerful/powerless fat-bodied and fat-brained consumer horde. As the stewardess floats farther up the aisle like a goddess riding a receding wave of consumer trash, I can tell several passengers want to applaud.

Part of me is hoping this is one of those moments where one person slow claps, then other people join in unison, and then the clapping speeds up until the frenetic energy takes over and people are screaming and showing their breasts in appreciation. Several airline passengers raise their hands, as to almost clap, and then adjust their hair or sit on their hands to touch their buttocks or put them in their pockets to play with their genitalia. Passengers don't applaud because they're cowards like me, and being a coward has something to do with our collective fear of death. Our daily cowardice comes from the somewhat rational/irrational belief that if we don't say anything or do anything particularly noticeable, maybe both our fellow mortals and God will forget we're around and not swiftly bring us our inevitable conclusion.

I should mention there is this other side of me that's not a coward. It's my animal-side, my wolf-side, and it's getting worse. This beast has no interest in reason. It only knows desire. My wolf-side has a different inclination completely in this moment and it definitely isn't to be unnoticeable. I have the nearly overwhelming desire to unzip my pants, wave my cock like a flag, and piss all over the aisle to mark my territory. After a glance at Fatty, I pull at my collar to get some air. He's less red now and I almost pity him.

"If you don't mind, where are you from, sir?" I ask.

Fatty wipes some sweat off his brow with his shirtsleeve and mutters, "Cincinnati."

TWO

HOMECOMING

I'm outside the only terminal of the Buffalo Niagara International Airport waiting for my cousin, Sal. Despite its international name, the airport is actually in the suburban town of Cheektowaga, where I grew up. Sal's late. He claims he doesn't have a cell phone these days. This strikes me as bullshit. Sal was a pot dealer in high school. In those days he had three pagers and was the first in the neighborhood to get a cell phone. No mobile device is supposed to indicate Sal's rehabilitated mentality. In our recent emails, he's also suggested some weird paranoia about government surveillance of his activities. We'll see how much he's changed. In my family, comfort with change is not one of our stronger evolutionary adaptations. We survived by having an extraordinary tough hide to weather life's storms.

It's January 2, 2015 and fucking freezing. Happy New Year. Like an idiot, I'm under dressed. I have on my Los Angeles winter coat, which is the seasonal equivalent of a fall jacket in Western New York. Sal Capella's my second cousin. Our fathers were first cousins, coming from my grandmother's side. Sal's a notorious degenerate. It's not entirely his fault. His father, Big Sal Capella, was a degenerate. Big Sal's father was a degenerate, too, and on it goes. My father carried the degenerate gene, but it was recessive.

Big Sal was never really around Little Sal much while he was growing up. Little Sal's mom, Audrey, divorced Big Sal when he was pretty young. When Big Sal did come around to play weekend warrior and make Audrey look like a shrew, he always had wads of cash. After our Little League games, I remember him buying all us kids ice cream at Mr. Frosty's and holding out his cash real high so all the baseball moms and dads could see it. It was about respect. He wanted it desperately.

I understand how Big Sal felt. I moved to Los Angeles to become a screenwriter. That was ten years ago. I've done a few projects where I received an actual paycheck. The great illusion of Hollywood is it's an industry with real paying jobs. If all capitalism is exploitative, then the industry of Hollywood ranks slightly above being murdered and made into food a la "Soylent Green."

For example, I did a rewrite of a Chinese horror movie called "Dead Head." It had nothing to do with the Grateful Dead. It may have been a better movie if that was the case. The writing experience certainly felt like a bad trip. The movie was about brain-eating aliens who landed in Los Angeles. I tried to turn it into social commentary about American culture. At first, the aliens became fat from consuming our bloated-with-bullshit-brains, but then they began to die off because, like Cheetos or Coke, our brains had no real nutritional value. The Chinese producers hated my version. I thought they, of all people, might appreciate my take on capitalism. Apparently, the Chinese love capitalism these days. I was paid out by the Chinese producers, actually half the pay I was owed, and summarily fired.

An Indian company just sacked me from another project – a

rewrite of a monster flick, werewolves and the like. The working title was "Blood Dog." Originally an Indian guy wrote it, I'm told. The execs claim a guild writer from the US had already done a rewrite before me. I find that pretty unlikely given the English-as-a-second-language feel to the entire thing, including the dialogue. The Indians proved no better to work with than the Chinese. I rewrote the hell out of the dialogue. They told me my re-written dialogue had an English-as-a-second-language feel to it. What the fuck? I didn't take their absurdity kindly. Lesson learned. Though there are more international bosses in Hollywood these days, bullshit remains the common currency.

Big Sal probably would have fared quite well in Hollywood. He had a big smile and gold teeth. Deep down, even he knew he was full of shit. With Little Sal, I'm not so sure of his bullshit awareness sometimes.

A car horn blasts. Except it's one of those specialty car horns and the horn's been programmed to ACDC's "Highway to Hell" so it sounds like "Honk, Honk, to Honk." Sal cruises up in a black, shiny, new, low-riding Dodge Ram pickup with plumes of cigarette smoke seeping out from his half-rolled down windows. Like father like…

"Tommy, how the hell are you?" Sal pulls over and hops out of the truck. He's a wily little fuck. "Let me have those." Before I can say anything, my bags are in the bed of his pickup.

"I'm all right."

"Get in."

And we're off. I study Sal's face. He looks old, anywhere between thirty and fifty. People age fast in Buffalo. They live hard. The weather is as rough as the economy. The funny thing about Los Angeles is no one really grows up. It's a city of transplanted vampires. Vapid blonde mid-western transplant after vapid blonde mid-western transplant feign disinterest in men and women alike while desperate for any type of actual human contact. These blonde vampire-types have lost the humanity they once took for granted in the mid-western towns of their youth. The undead transplants now living on the West Side cradle their yoga mats like human babies. And I'm one of them about as much as I was one of them from Sal's and my high school, which is to say utterly and not at all. There are deep lines etched below Sal's eyes, and if there's one thing I've learned about lines, they tell a story whether you step on them, jump over them, snort them, or have the courage to write them down. Sal's eyes tell a story that's as worthy as any. That's why I moved to Los Angeles. I wanted to tell the story of my people. That and to get the hell out of Western New York.

"How is she?" I ask.

Sal looks right at me. He knows the "she" I'm referring to is Camilla. Sal's an expert in avoidance. I can almost respect it. People who become great at something, however esoteric or annoying, impress me. Avoidance is also a personal area of expertise. It must run in the family, that and our leathery asses.

"How do you like her?" Sal asks regarding his truck. "She's brand new."

"You working?"

Sal can feel the judgment seeping out of my words. He may be a degenerate but that doesn't make him insensitive. "I landscape. You know, when the weather's better."

"That's like two months of the year," I say.

"She's got power. She's got a lot of burst."

"I bet."

"How's your work?" Sal fires back. "Writing any movies?"

It's hard to be a writer and hardly ever get paid to write. You develop a tolerance for pain when people ask what film you're working on, and you have nothing to offer them. I parlay his strike easily. "Truck's real nice, Sal. Lots of pick-up. I'm happy for you."

Sal's out of the airport driving down Genesee Street, and then down Transit Road. It's a funny thing. I notice changes on these old, busy streets – little things, like that gas station is new or the McDonald's has moved two blocks from where I remember it. There are some strip malls that feel a little less full to me than when I was last here several years ago, but then, there are also a few newer ones that seem to be doing well enough. I can't help but keep thinking about that McDonald's.

"Why'd that McDonald's move?" I ask.

"What do you mean?"

"What's the reason it moved?"

"It just did."

"Well, it didn't relocate itself in the middle of the night for no purpose."

"You want me to turn around and get you a coffee or something?" Sal asks.

"No. Thanks."

"You think too much about stuff that don't matter."

"Agreed."

One time this Polish kid in middle school was bullying Sal. There were a lot more Polish kids than Italian kids in Cheektowaga in those days. Sal and I looked so alike, two scrawny Italian kids, that some days I'd take the brunt of it on Sal's behalf. All of a sudden, I'd get pushed against the locker and when I'd gather myself the assailant would be only a shadow of fading laughter running down the hall. Kids can be cruel when you're different. Sal and I aren't so different these days either. The two of us remain kids wishing our fathers were still around and they were better men. We wish we were better men, too. The dark circles under our eyes make us look kind of like twins. Only my story's been basking in a constant sun, and his has been buried deep down under a perpetual winter. Maybe we've both been buried all these years under the weight of a past we can't ever quite escape, whether you build a house upon it or smash it down and drive three days straight to Los Angeles.

We drive into my old neighborhood in a part of town called South Cheektowaga. Cheektowaga is a Seneca Indian word; it means "Land of the Crabapples." We haven't seen any Seneca Indians around here for a while, but I was told in elementary school they existed and the name of the town is proof. These days we have a bunch of Polish people sprinkled with the occasional German or Italian family. Cheektowaga's a place where these distinctions matter, mostly in terms of the drinking holidays. The Polish take care of Dyngus Day; the Italians, Columbus Day. There aren't enough Germans to really make Oktoberfest a big deal.

Sal's attention fixes on a teenage girl and boy walking up the sidewalk toward my mom's house. He slows down so we can get a real good look at them. The girl is holding a casserole. They stare back at us. The girl waves and I give her a nod. Sal speeds up.

"The neighborhood's shit now. Fucking Mexicans are taking over," Sal says.

"I don't think they're Mexican."

"What are they then?"

"I don't know. Not that it matters, but they look like they could be Indians."

"Bows and arrows."

"They don't use… No. From India."

Sal shrugs off the Indians. He's not a racist idiot, but he plays the part.

"It's different now," he says.

We're on my mom's street – Crabapple Court. It must've been the developer's idea. There are crabapple trees in front of each house. Some people have the erroneous belief that they are particularly poisonous. Don't get me wrong, they're toxic little bastards. It's true that crabapples have low doses of cyanide in their seeds, but so do regular apples. Crabapples won't hurt you unless you eat a ton of them. They're disgustingly tart, so who'd want to in any case?

"Really. Why don't you have a cell? Given your nature, I find that hard to believe."

"Given my... Goddamn government's listening to every-fucking-thing."

I egg him on, "Really? And the Mexicans are taking over Cheektowaga?"

We pull into my mom's driveway and park.

"You mean, the Indians?"

"Yes."

"Patriot Act," Sal says with a straight face.

He is so sincere I think for a second maybe he is onto something. Above us I hear the not-too-distant sound of a propeller plane. There's a little private airport about a mile and a half away. I wonder if it's a government spy plane and it's up there watching this homecoming. My mom's crabapple tree, dead center in the front yard, catches my eye. It's had this unhealthy look for years and it's still pretty moribund. But apparently that little toxic tree won't give up the ghost, not easily anyway.

I glance up to see the door creak open. There she is, the great lady herself, Camilla D'Angelo. She's bent over some and her wizened limbs are hanging a little lower to the earth. Camilla's smiling her toothy smile and it reminds me of a grin I've seen before when she's especially pleased with herself. Her little crabapple branch arms wave us in.

It's not until that moment I really look down the street and notice all the cars parked in front of our house. Then, I see that Indian girl and boy walking up the driveway past me. My mother ushers them into the house. She's thrown a surprise homecoming party. For a moment, I dream there are lots of crabapples growing on the tree and eat them all. Sal punches me on the shoulder and says, "She's your mom. Throwing you a party makes her happy."

"I know."

Sal gets out of the truck first. I stay for a moment to take one last deep breath before I plunge into my homecoming.

THREE
LET'S PARTY LIKE IT'S 1999

Camilla hugs me tight in the foyer as she wetly kisses me square on the lips. I'd wipe off the slobber but she has me in a maternal wrestling move and my arms are pinned to my sides. I try to wriggle free but, sick or not, she's pretty strong. I've never once questioned my mother's strength. If anything, she's a force of often misapplied nature. Let me set this straight. I love my mother, yet her presence revolts me a little. You're probably thinking to yourself, I'm a teenage boy who never grew up. Well, let me tell you something then, we're all inconsolable teenage boys, and that's not just a Buffalo or Cheektowaga thing, or even a man thing – it's an "us" thing. It's a human condition thing.

The veins in her hands bulge as Camilla squeezes my paws. She looks pretty healthy to me, considering. Back in Los Angeles, Camilla informed me the doctors don't know why her body is failing her again. In this context, "again" is the scariest word. About ten years ago, Camilla had an "episode." The doctors described it as such because they were not able to identify the initial happening that caused her subsequent illness. Camilla suddenly and completely lost all her fine motor skills. She had to learn to talk and walk again. With the support of my father, Frank, she made quite the recovery. Dad saw Camilla well and then he died of a heart attack in the garage while starting the snow blower. That was five years ago. Life and death are strange.

Now, ten years after Camilla's original incident, there are only slight hitches in her speech and walk that give away all she's been through. Her organs are shutting down, and the doctors have no answers, again. Camilla's had enough, she told me. At this point, the doctors think she may have mere months to live, but they don't know for sure. Death is the only certainty they're offering. It doesn't make sense. How can my mother's body and mind fall apart, be rebuilt piece by piece, and then her most vital organs break down once more, bit by bit? None of Camilla's doctors know anything to really help her, or even offer her information to better understand why her vessel has malfunctioned twice so thoroughly. That's how it is in this world. Being alone and in pain is clear, yet no one can explain our condition to us. We fight like dogs to persevere and then once we've defeated the biggest dog we've ever seen, another shows up twice as large. Camilla does, indeed, look well, considering.

I'm not ready for Camilla to not be around to dote on me and make me feel so abundantly over-loved. Camilla's a fighter. But she wouldn't have asked me to come and help unless this felt like the end. She purses her lips and makes a disapproving utterance only Catholic moms can make. Believe me, I've tried to replicate it and I just don't have the capacity on account I'm not a mom and I'm a lapsed Catholic. You have to remember her speech is a little slow and stilted due to the remnants of her previous condition. "What… kind…of…coat…is…that?"

"The only one I have, Mom."

Before I can mount a counterattack, Camilla's taking the coat off me and putting it in the closet. I'm suddenly eight years old again and I just came in from building a snow fort in the front yard to protect the neighborhood from Soviet invaders. Back then, when Camilla said I was pretending to be something, I'd always say I wasn't pretending. So, she'd say *you're pretending to be a fireman.* I'd glare back, *I am a fireman. How dare you? Don't you see my red wagon is a fire truck?* I was a serious kid. Not much has changed.

"You can borrow one of your father's. I'm so happy you're here. Everyone's here to see you. Can you believe it?"

"Can I help with anything?"

Camilla waves me off and makes that disapproving sound again. "Relax. I'm fine. Everyone's helping."

With that, Camilla's off and entertaining. Even now, she is a force. Camilla's right. Everyone's at this party. The entire neighborhood. People I haven't seen in years. Some I thought were already dead. I guess they're still kicking. People I haven't met before are here, too. There are a couple of young families with their kids running around the house playing tag.

Geez… I didn't realize Camilla had the pull to get this many people over to the house. For a minute, I dare to think that maybe they've heard I'm a big Hollywood person and they've all come to see me. But nobody's paying me any attention – how very Hollywood of these Cheektowagans. And then, I see Camilla putting on a show as she directs the Indians to the table with all the food and beckons them to eat. Her hands rise and fall dramatically like Liz Turner in "Cleopatra," as she points out all the typical Buffalo fare: pizza, wings, blue cheese, and Frank's Hot Sauce. She offers the kids what we call "pop" and everyone else in the country refers to as "soda," as she guides them away from a couple boxes of wine on the table and the Labatt Blue beers in the cooler.

Everyone is here for Camilla. She's the star. It's not because she's dying. It's because she's always been the star and the center of everything, whether in our home, in the neighborhood, or in every known and unknown universe.

My uncles. Oh my god, my uncles are here! Uncle Tony (Uncle T) and Uncle Spider (nick-named after the Marvel hero or because he always claims to have a spider bite on his ass and threatens to show it) have been feuding for decades. They're talking together in the corner like nothing's the matter. Uncle Spider voraciously shakes my hand as he pulls me in close. He speaks like a chainsaw in need of a tune-up, "Your mom's happy you're home, kid."

"I'm glad to be here, Uncle Spider, considering."

Uncle T nods knowingly and leans in, "You look skinny."

"I eat every ten days like a snake."

"Have a slice of pepperoni," Uncle T says.

Sal weighs in, "He don't eat meat."

Where the fuck did Sal come from? He's like this fart I had once at the Playboy Mansion. Okay, it was a house party several blocks away. The flatulence didn't smell malodorous until a hot brunette engaged me in classy conversation. Actually, she asked me where the bathroom was so she could blow some coke and I had a bad falafel earlier in the day in Beverly Hills. To be totally transparent, I actually ate it at a sketchy stand in Highland Park. I think the owner of the falafel stand was Mexican, by the way.

"What?" Uncle T asks in total confusion.

My ears perk at the gradual increasing sound of a propeller plane. Could this be the same one from when we were outside?

"He's a vegetarian," Sal says.

"Sal doesn't use a cell because he thinks the government's spying on him," I tattle back.

"Smart man," Uncle Spider says, as we all hear the plane fly right over the house and each of us has this weird Pavlovian response and automatically looks up.

"God, the Bills are disappointing this year," says Uncle T. "You watch any games out there in California? I hear the quarterback's a vegetarian."

For those unfamiliar, Uncle T's talking about the Buffalo Bills.

They are the professional football team that lost four Super Bowls in a row during my formative years in the early nineties. Furthermore, the Bills haven't made the playoffs in the last fifteen years. Whenever I hear someone talk about the Bills, I have the instinctual desire to protect my testicles because the Bills are a constant kick in the nuts. I hate the Bills and I totally love them more than any woman I've lived with. I'm totally obsessed about the Bills. I go on Buffalo Bills Backers boards online and argue with fans about what being a real fan is about. In case you're wondering, it's about loyalty – even when reason and mental health suggest otherwise. Watching the games is compulsory. If I don't, I feel guilt. It's like Catholic guilt but worse. If I do watch the Bills, I get sick to my stomach. "First of all, the quarterback's a pescatarian. In any case, I doubt that was his problem slinging the rock, Uncle T. I think we can blame the porous O-line and not his avoiding hamburger meat." Uncle T gapes at me like I've just been sacked by a gargantuan nose tackle and my body's all mangled. I shouldn't have used the words pescatarian or porous.

Uncle Spider starts to pull down his pants to lighten the mood. "Would you like to see this spider bite I got? It's huge."

Camilla waves me over from across the way. She's talking to a moderately attractive young woman with a jock-looking guy beside her. Their ease-with-each-other meets touch-of-desperation gives away they're married. By moderately attractive, I mean she's thin. By jock-looking, I mean he has biceps larger than his rotund beer gut. Life turns to slow motion. Do I enter into Camilla's snake pit or stay and get a good look at my uncle's wrinkly ass? Life speeds up to double-time. I bolt for it and look back to see the horrified look on Sal's face, as he's too slow to avoid my uncle's spider bite. Serves him right.

Camilla makes the introductions; I smile and nod. This couple's only been in the neighborhood for a few years. He's a truck driver for a milk company. She's a pre-school teacher. Right away, I can tell this guy doesn't like me. The feeling's mutual. What a dick. He reminds me of the jock basketball player who only talks to you once throughout all of high school to brag about the triple/double he scored at the big game. Fuck this milkman. Then I learn why the milkman is on edge as Camilla goes off on how Mrs. Preschool Teacher used to do some acting in high school. Apparently, she was Peter Pan. I smile, nod, and can tell her husband's getting pissed. He's sweating and tapping his foot. Camilla says, "Maybe you can put her in one of your films someday." The preschool teacher blushes.

I play it up, "That's a great idea, Mom." The milkman whisks the preschool teacher away.

Camilla leans in. "He cheats on her. The piece of shit. She could use a friend."

I love it when Camilla swears. That's because she does so infrequently and really makes the most of it by enunciating each profane word. "She's married, Mom."

"I only said she could use a friend."

Part of me wishes Camilla faked her illness to get me to come home so she could play matchmaker. It's a nice thought.

I see Sal from a distance staring at the Indian girl. Her hair is long and black. She has the kind of beauty that doesn't age away. I imagine her at sixty years old and it's all still there, and not buried deep down either, but right on the surface. That beauty has something to do with the mind and the spirit. It's cultivated internally and manifests outward. That's the sort of beauty I'm looking for. I'm guessing the girl's about sixteen or seventeen. Noticing her beauty is not perverted. In my view, it's only perverse if I do something untoward.

"That's Priya. Her family moved into the Polaks' old place a couple of years back."

"The Pollocks?" I ask wryly. My father always referred to Polish people as pollocks. I never wanted to turn into my father and here I am, trying to make the same poor taste ethnic jokes to get a rise out of my mom. Camilla never approved of those jokes. I truly don't remember the Polaks, by the way.

My mom gently smacks me on the hand for my intentional mispronunciation. "No. The Polaks. It was the Caminskis' place. Then the Polaks'. Now Priya's family lives there. They're the Vaswanis."

Camilla's talking about the corner house two doors down. I remember the Caminskis. They were old to me even when I was growing up, and their kids were out of the house by the time I was looking for playmates. The only thing I remember is Mrs. Caminski obsessed about her grass, and if you dared to try to retrieve a ball that ended up in her back yard by hopping the fence, she'd scream at you in this low-voice like a total psycho.

"Oh, I see," I say.

"Priya's going to the University of Buffalo next year. She's very smart. Her brother's name is Neel. Their parents are back in India for a couple of weeks, so I look in on her and Neel from time to time. Priya's very sweet. Too young for you, but very sweet." Priya looks over at us perceptibly. I bet she even knows my inner thoughts. Priya reminds me of the reason I left Buffalo for Los Angeles. I was on a quest to find her sort of beauty. "I think Neel's going to be an engineer like his dad."

Sal makes his way over to Neel and slaps him on the shoulder. That seems a bit familiar. He acted like he didn't know Neel and Priya before. At first glance, Neel doesn't look much like a soon-to-be engineer. His clothes are baggy and his hair is in a mohawk. He looks like a typical, lost suburban kid. Maybe I'm wrong. Judging people is not my greatest strength. Camilla and I both watch as Uncle Spider chugs one beer while offering another to Priya and Neel. Mom moves rather quickly into action to rescue them. She's become a superhero over the years at rescuing innocents from her well-intentioned but totally crazed brother.

A firm hand lands on my shoulder. I spin around to see my old pal Vic Carruso. It's been fifteen years since I last saw him. He's enormous, and I don't mean obese. Vic's a huge weight lifter. He brought his whole family with him including his wife Charlene and his five little kids, Vic Junior, Victoria, Vincent, Vivian, and Miriam. They're all beautiful and sweet. Vic hugs me. His wife, who I've never met before, hugs me. All the kids line up like a platoon of well-behaved soldiers and shake my hand. Each one of them gives me eye contact and refers to me as Mr. Tommy. Can you believe it?

The funny thing about Vic is we were always close even though we didn't really hang out much in high school. I personally blame the school for putting us in different classes and charting out our radically different lives. Maybe we always liked each other simply because he was a nice guy and I guess I was, too. That might not seem like much of a basis for friendship, but niceness is an underrated quality in high school, and everywhere for that matter. In some ways, our lives now are as different as they can be. He's a family man with kids and he's a respectable pharmacist. I'm a divorcee married to my floundering screenwriting career. In other ways, Vic and I are exactly the same. We both are still sincere, even after all these years. When Vic says something, he means it. It's the same way with me. I can't help it. Camilla's sincere, too, and she really cares about people. It's in my DNA. That's why I've taken an interest in Priya. My mom cares about her so I do, too. That's the only reason.

It's the end of the evening as Camilla and I say goodbye to our last guests, Uncle T and Uncle Spider. Uncle T's holding up Uncle Spider by his belt on account he had a few too many Labatts. Uncle Spider keeps trying to pull down his pants.

"I've got to take a leak," Uncle Spider slurs.

"You'll have to help him, T," Camilla commands. Knowing my mom like I do, I think she's very much enjoying this predicament. But she plays it straight. I admire the choice.

"Fine," Uncle T grits.

One step at a time, Uncle T escorts Uncle Spider to the bathroom.

Camilla and I have a moment alone. She holds up her hand to stop me from saying anything. It's as if she knows exactly what's about to happen.

"For the love of Christ, he's pissing all over my leg!"

Camilla lets out the loudest belly laugh and I can tell she's really happy. And I'm happy she's happy.

I really am. The complicated relationship between Uncle T and Uncle Spider I found previously mysterious is also much clearer now.

Camilla places her hand in her pocket. She's holding something there.

Being an only child wasn't the plan. It's just Camilla couldn't have any more kids. She definitely tried and had several miscarriages. The lost children never left her really; Mom did her duty and carried them along. We all did, even me in the way only a son could. I knew she was suffering and no matter what I did, I could not help the pain abate. Even my father felt her pain and, it seemed at times to me, he hardly felt anything. Eventually, Catholic or not, Dad put his foot down. Enough was enough.

Good Catholics, like Mom and Dad, can be suckers for suffering. But for my father that was only to a point, whereas Camilla would go the entire way. After Camilla's last miscarriage, my father mandated that he didn't want any crucifixes in the house. He claimed the gore creeped him out. It became a battle between him and my mother. Camilla didn't want the neighbors to stop over and think we were Protestants or worse.

I can still remember one time when Frank returned home from

work to find a crucifix hanging in the kitchen. He looked up from grabbing a beer and there was Jesus staring down at him. I must have been about thirteen. Man, did Dad howl. He left the house and didn't come home until morning. By the time he returned, it was gone. My mother never copped to taking the crucifix down and I didn't touch it. I doubt Jesus decided to move to another residence on his own, but I can understand if he was tempted, given all the fighting regarding his presence.

Camilla didn't mind suffering so much. I think in some way she felt most alive holding onto it. Even now, at Camilla's most jovial, there's sadness hidden in the crevices of her eyes and the corners of her mouth. It's always there. That pain. The feeling of so many lost years and all the children she couldn't hold onto. They were gone before they were ever really here.

Uncle T escorts Uncle Spider out of the bathroom. There's a wet spot on his leg. Camilla and I don't dare smile.

Camilla pulls two rosaries out of her pocket. "T, Spider, I want you to have these."

I remember these rosaries. When I was a kid of about ten, I was snooping around in my parent's bedroom on a mission to figure out who these people really were. They claimed to have created me, but I wasn't certain I believed them. How did they live? What secrets did they keep? Were they hiding treasure in their bedroom?

After finding the rosaries, I brought them to Camilla. That's when she told me the story that these very rosaries were made from the cross that hung Christ. Even then, I had trouble believing. First of all, why would you want these rosaries if they were made from the thing that killed Jesus? Secondly, how could these relics end up in my mother's jewelry box in Cheektowaga?

The truth, I think, was she had been lied to by her mother, so she lied to me. Additionally, a priest probably lied to my grandmother when he gave her the rosaries in the first place. I suppose that's how religion begins. But far be it for me to tarnish the reputation of priests or the genesis of religion in general. The priests have hurt their standing themselves, and my only qualification to critique religion is a writer's cynicism.

What Camilla had in her favor as a storyteller was a stubbornness of the highest quality. Come to think of it, perhaps that's how religion really gains traction, unabashed stubbornness and a knack for sustaining tall tales in the faces of questioning children.

Uncle T pockets the rosaries for both him and Uncle Spider. In a gentle tone he says, "Thank you, Camilla." The worry in his voice and the lump in my throat makes me more fully aware of the resolute fact that my mother is dying.

"I'm tired, honey," Camilla whispers.

I watch Camilla walk up the stairs. She's frail. Mom moves slowly and grips the railing with each step. My father did the same thing right before he died. I allow myself to dream that he's at the top of the stairs waiting for her. He's a little annoyed because she's moving at a snail's pace and he refuses to go to bed without her, even after all these years. Neurotic or not, selfish or not, it's sweet.

A streetlight sneaks in from the bay window to steal my memory. The light hits Camilla's face funny as she turns and looks at me. It's like I'm watching her ghost. She makes it to the hallway and she's gone. I suppose she made it into her room. My hand appears paler than before. It could be the streetlight or the fact I'm scared and exhausted. Somehow, I've changed during this party. It's like a part of me is disappearing, and an inchoate part of me is finally being born.

FOUR

BORN AGAIN

The four-legged creature scurries from the bushes in front of the house in the midnight hour. It's ebony like the absolute night. But its blackness does not suggest anything evil, just something primordial, moribund, and unknowable. A shaggy mane flows from the scruff of its neck. It's like a wolf but much larger. The creature gnaws at the crabapple tree in front of the house with teeth like scissors. Perhaps it's trying to wear down its ferocious fangs. The animal then sticks its claws in the tree to test either the tree's strength or its claws'. It's the sort of behavior one does when bored. The claw becomes stuck and breaks free after what must have felt like a panicked eternity. Freedom! The animal runs around the front yard like a dog expending every last bit of its energy before crashing for the night. It yelps as one of its paws sticks in the mud and sprains. The beast holds its wounded paw to the moon in hopes that its only friend, celestial or otherwise, might bear witness to its undignified suffering. The withholding lunar monstrosity offers the same stoic response as ever – abject indifference. The animal lowers its head, dejected, or offering a prayer.

Boom. Boom. Boom boom! Boom boom! Boom boom boom boom!

Oh my God! My heart is racing. I'm alive! Holy fuck I'm alive. Where the fuck am I? What the fuck is going on? I exist!

It's okay. I'm okay. It must be morning as the light is shining onto the bed. I'm in my childhood bedroom. How I arrived is an utter mystery. Camilla has morphed my old bedroom into an arts and crafts area. There's a desk with some doilies and shit on it. Camilla makes these things to pass the time. When I was a kid, I tried to hone my capitalism, and get her to sell them and give me a percentage. We didn't have many sales.

Some of the old remnants from my youth remain in the room. There are Buffalo Sabres and Buffalo Bills pennants on the walls. I was a big local sports fan. If I wasn't playing street football with the neighborhood kids, I was playing street hockey. We always pretended we played for the Sabres or the Bills. Come to think of it, it says a lot about my upbringing that we were allowed to play contact sports on the street. Not one parent or other concerned citizen ever told us to get out of the street and take our little asses to the park. I come from a hearty, foolish people.

The particulars of the manner I made it to bed last night are disconcerting. I wasn't drunk or otherwise under the influence. Worrying about it won't solve anything. Don't stress about the heart-racing thing, either. This is the way I wake up every morning. I call it a neurotic fear of both life and death. My mind is like Woody Allen on amphetamine doing cartwheels on stilts. In my sleep, I dream anxious dreams about life. When I wake up, I'm totally freaked out that I'm going to die. It's easy to say that only hyper-smart, aware people have this issue. But honestly, if I could be two steps intellectually slower and not be so stressed out, I'd stick a beer helmet on my head and happily run the average race while chugging a brew. Okay, that's not entirely honest, but it's how I feel sometimes.

In terms of honesty about my intelligence, I think I'm smart but not overly. My IQ is probably at the bare minimum necessary to really do something with one's life, given one has enough luck to be ready for those few opportunities we really have. Unfortunately, somewhere in my adolescence I convinced myself art was not only socially viable for a lower to middle class kid like me, but also an entirely worthwhile enterprise for both self and society. I don't think this idea is entirely wrongheaded. Coming from where I do, books and films probably saved my life. They made me feel less alone at those times when so did the idea of death.

I am talking about the idea of death here, not the definite finality of it. Actual suicide has never been appealing, but I became very sad as a teenager. This sadness carried over into my twenties and thirties. It's like a fiercely loyal, dark friend who can never be ditched. When I used to be especially sad, occasionally the idea of death comforted me. Sometimes the notion of death felt peaceful – like death could be stepping into nothing when the suffering something of life kept gnawing at the brain and bones. Thoughts of death do not comfort me anymore. As I've grown older and experienced life and all the awful beautiful pain and joy of it, I cling to life like it's a mast and I'm in the middle of a sea in the fiercest storm.

Also, in terms of honesty, I want to be straight about something. Before bed, I had a couple glasses of wine. There's a bit of gray area on this point where it's possible I may have had several glasses. Regardless, my drinking was well within my normal limits, so I absolutely did not black out from alcohol consumption and crawl up the stairs into my old bed unknowingly. As I mentioned previously, I value honesty above all other qualities. I try to straighten the record when I feel I've been unclear. To me, feelings, when truly expressed, are pretty honest little things even though they are sort of fleeting, mental fabrications as opposed to the actual facts of an event.

Right now, I feel pain. It's in my ankle, and it's sharp. I stand up and inspect my leg. There's a deep, already purpling bruise covering my foot. This is very distressing. What the hell did I do last night? I look around the room for something that might comfort me. When I was a kid, I used to have a hockey stick I always kept in the corner near the closet. My father gave it to me. When I was twelve-years-old, I had it autographed by a Czechoslovakian Sabres' player named Richard Smehlik. The Sabres had this "Shoot, Pass, and Skate Competition" at the old Memorial Auditorium. It was free to the public, so it gave lots of working class families a chance to see the Sabres up close. My father took me. After, he told me where to stand outside to get an autograph. I was terrified. When Smehlik came out of the stadium, that we all referred to as the Aud, he was the biggest man I'd ever seen. I asked for his autograph. He was very nice and signed it. Smehlik wasn't my favorite player, but he was available for an autograph and that was enough. That stick became my most prized possession. I never played with it for fear it would be damaged. What the hell happened to that stick? My body feels like I played a double overtime hockey game last night. God, I'm sore.

I smell burnt coffee downstairs.

Camilla's making us breakfast. She knows exactly how I like my eggs, sunny side up. Of course, she never makes them that way due to the fact she's an awful cook. She's nearly finished with my scrambled eggs. I say *my* scrambled eggs because Camilla doesn't ever eat them. The eggs run like all bloody hell down the pan. Even they want to flee from breakfast, and they're the damned breakfast. It's not that Camilla doesn't try. She just doesn't have the skill.

Cooking, like art, is a matter of feel. Some people have the feel for cooking. Some people have the feel for eating good cooking. Some people just cook and eat to survive. Some people cook and eat to survive but don't even know that's what they're doing. I suppose you can expand that metaphor outward exponentially about everything provided that you're into metaphors. Camilla is blissfully unaware that she can't cook nor does she have the taste to know she's eating terrible food.

For my part, I have come to terms with that fact regarding my mom. Camilla can't cook and has no real taste, but she was never withholding of feeling or time. She invested fully in me as a child. I was her only and she gave me whatever capacities she did have. She read to me as a child, and often. Later, when I began to get in a creative mode, she let me tell her the stories I made up. I suppose, the time for my telling her my stories has mostly passed but every once in a while I share with her something I'm writing and she understands the heart of it.

The urge to take over the egg-making is nearly overwhelming. Camilla seems happy so I show restraint and pour myself some coffee instead.

"Sit down already. Let me serve you," she bosses.

"You've been serving everyone since I came in."

"I like to do it."

I know she's right, so I plop down at the dining room table. Within eye-line are the front yard and the crabapple tree. I can see animal tracks all over the snow. Camilla puts the eggs and toast on a plate.

"Please, Mom. Tell me what the doctors are saying."

Camilla sighs heavily and looks out the window. I think she sees the tracks, too. "Three months. It could be more."

Mom turns and examines me. She must see the pain in my eyes. "There's nothing else they can do?"

Camilla sits and holds my hand like I'm a child. "No. My body's had enough. But it's okay, honey. It really is."

"I'm staying with you, here."

"I can't have you putting your life on hold."

"I won't be. I can write here. Spending time with you isn't wasted time."

A couple of tears make it halfway down Camilla's face before she wipes them away. She gently smacks me on the face. "You're a good boy."

I look into my mother's eyes and see her when she was thirty-six years old. She's always been that age to me. Then I look out on the crabapple tree again and at the strange tracks all around it. I wish I could start living my life over again. Maybe I'd do things differently. Maybe not. But we'd have more time.

A person is supposed to have life figured out by the age of thirty-seven. That's one year older than the age I always remember my own mother. I never thought thirty-seven was attainable, yet here I am. Camilla and I need time to sort my life out.

The crucifix on the wall is a little crooked. Camilla hung it after my father died, not out of spite, but to remember him. Their battles over hanging crucifixes were really an expression of their love. Dad hurt because she hurt and he just wanted the pain to go away for both of them. His idea about pain was simple: you don't hang it on the wall. Her idea was simple too, you never forget. And, hanging in the balance between them, there was always love. I see the crabapple tree swaying in the wind in an attempt to divert attention from the animal tracks in the snow.

The tree's a funny little albatross, monstrosity savior. It's delicate but not, and could be a religion unto itself. Those mean roots run deep. They hold earth more ancient than the oldest religions. There are bright fairies and demons down there, all singing and dancing together to keep the world spinning. I look up at Jesus again and the pained look on his face turns into something else. Perhaps he's almost smiling. Somehow, I feel a little born again. Can you be a little born again? I surely hope so.

FIVE
THE NEIGHBORHOOD'S CHANGED

Camilla kicked me out of the house. Not permanently. She strongly suggested I take a very long walk because she thinks I'm treating her like an invalid. I was trying to fix the door handle to the bathroom. It was loose and I was afraid it was going to fall off. Also, I hate the idea of bathroom doors that don't lock properly. It's my belief a bathroom is a sacred space – a place where one ought to feel some relative assurance no one will enter unexpectedly.

I learned the spiritual importance of bathrooms from my father. The man entered with a newspaper as soon as he came home from work and exited no less than one hour later. On the other hand, Camilla never appreciated the significance of a sacrosanct bathroom space. She still doesn't. Camilla's always trying to talk to people when she's in the bathroom, or talk to people when they're in the bathroom. She's just always talking. So, Camilla caught me tightening the doorknob with a kitchen knife and that was it. According to her, I'd crossed a boundary. Her exact words, "You're sullying a kitchen knife. How dare you treat me like an invalid. I've been maintaining restroom door knobs since before I created your very being." Okay, those weren't her exact words.

As a writer, I like to slightly elevate common language in my dialogue. My argument for doing so is if we wanted to hear regular people talk regularly we'd talk to the actual real people in our lives rather than go to the movies. As an example, I give you Colonel Jessep in "A Few Good Men," played by the venerable Jack Nicholson. Remember when he's on trial and the world's most lovable/detestable scientology zealot, Tom Cruise, is breaking him down with his solicitor skills?

Jessep grimaces mid-monologue. "And my existence, while grotesque and incomprehensible to you, saves lives. You don't want the truth because deep down in places you don't talk about at parties, you want me on that wall, you need me on that wall." Jessep doesn't talk like a regular Joe down at the bar complaining about the state of the Buffalo Bills, and I could listen to him for hours. Undoubtedly, he's an asshole, but he's a lovable asshole because at least he's interesting.

Speaking of lovable assholes, I'm reminded of this kid I grew up with named Derek. When we were in the neighborhood playing street hockey, he developed an amazing strategy to get around the general rule parents have about profanity. His mother didn't want him to refer to everyone on the street as an asshole, but he really loved saying asshole above all other swears. To get around her mandate – and this was even when she was nowhere near earshot – he referred to all of us assholes as "ess-ohs." Like, stop being such an ess-oh, ess-oh. He constantly spoke like this from the fourth to sixth grades. She-hate stood in for shit. Fuck became fa-duck. I respected Derek because he pushed the limit. He feared his mom, but not too much. That said, I've never been a fan of mean assholes.

There's Derek's old house across the street. He wasn't an asshole really; he was just a regular guy. Derek's long gone now. By long gone I mean he grew up and moved three streets over to an off-white colonial that looks just like this one. I sort of think that might be a great thing. If a person feels so good about their upbringing, and they make the conscious choice to recreate that environment for their own children, then I am the first person to pat them on the back and say, "right on." I just can't bring myself to respect people who don't make choices.

When the snow melts, lots of debris floats down the sewer grates on this very street. Sometimes the grates clog. I remember my father on his hands and knees unclogging the sewer drain so the street wouldn't flood. At the end of the day, the debris is unconscious trash floating down murky water. That's all it is. No more, no less. There's no reason to respect unconscious trash. And I'm not saying people are trash. I am saying some people act like trash sometimes.

Neither Camilla nor I have lived with someone else for a long time. I haven't been married for about four years, and I haven't cohabited with a girlfriend for a couple. My father's been gone now for five years. It's funny how you can get used to living with someone but can get used to living without them, too.

I always liked taking walks around the block as a kid. As I look back to the house for a moment, I can picture my father puttering out in the front yard, snow-shoveling the driveway. But he's not a ghost, just a distant memory. According to Sal, the neighborhood's changed so much. At first glance, it doesn't look like it's changed at all. A dog sprints up to me from the house on the corner behind a fence that could use a paint job. That fence could have used that same paint job twenty years back. The dog's a doughy, yellow lab. He cocks his head and stares at me like I'm an alien.

This hot girl, Farrah, used to live here. Her mom and dad were big hippies. The first time I met Farrah she was doing yoga with her parents in their back yard. I had hopped the fence to retrieve a football, and there she was stretching elegantly. She was five years older than me. Farrah had long, dirty-blonde hair and I remember she was a dancer. She watched me once when my parents were out for an evening. I guess you could say she was my babysitter. She was seventeen and I was twelve. Farrah took a shower when I was over and came out only wearing a white towel. She was fucking with me. I was too young to do anything about it. If she had dropped that towel, I would have been absolutely one-hundred percent terrified. Thankfully, she didn't. But deep down I immediately felt more grown-up. I knew enough to know she wanted my attention.

It was probably creepy for her to do what she did. She was almost a woman and I wasn't even close to being a man. I'd like to let her off the hook completely and say we're all animals but I never did anything like that to a girl five years younger than me when I was her age. Still, Farrah taught me something. I always looked at her as this unattainable goddess. But, from that moment on, I knew sometimes what feels unattainable and what you can really attain can change in an instant.

Where is Farrah now? Does she still look like a dancer? If she followed her parents' fleshy trajectory, I doubt it. I mean no disrespect to her or her parents, truly. Suddenly, I'm feeling all nostalgic and have this warmth emanating from my body and the dog's looking at me demurely like he might really love me or something. I stick my hand over the fence to pat his gentle head. The dog snaps at me and barks his head off. I see his fangs, but don't flinch. On instinct, I lunge toward the fence and show my teeth. The dog backs away and I do, too. I taste something sulfurous in my mouth. It's my blood. I must have bitten my lip.

We used to have a dog named Jack when I was growing up. Jack was really my father's. Frank loved that dog. My father named the dog after Jack Kemp, the Buffalo Bills quarterback. For those who don't know, Jack Kemp was the quarterback of the Buffalo Bills from 1962 to 1969. He led the Bills to two American Football

League Championships. My father loved Jack Kemp like he was his own son. They were almost the same age, so that was a bit odd. After Jack Kemp retired, he became a politician and ran for congress in the old 31st Congressional District in Western New York. My father voted for him every election he was able to. There were some elections when he couldn't because the state kept changing the boundaries of our district.

Our Jack was a goofy lab-mix and mostly a happy dog. That said, he didn't take any shit. I think he had some Doberman in him. My father broke his ankle at work when I was eleven so I was the man of the house. Frank was out of work for six months; money was tight; there was work to be done, and I had to step up. People act like childhood is something to be stretched out, but I don't regret growing up fast. It was my responsibility to take Jack on all the walks while my father recovered. Unbeknownst to me, Jack had serious tension with a dog on the other side of the block. So, I walked Jack around the block in front of enemy territory. From behind sinister bushes and a fence, the other dog erupted in barks. Jack was not going to take that bullshit. Our otherwise happy-go-lucky dog totally lost his mind.

Vicious sounds came out from Jack. He lunged toward the fence, nearly ripping off my eleven-year-old arm. Foam sprayed from his mouth. The other dog ran up and down the fence and Jack took off chasing him. Jack was a ninety-pound dog. At the time, I weighed eighty-five pounds. Before I knew what was happening, I was flying through the air. Then I was on the ground and Jack dragged me along the sidewalk. At that point, I still had the leash in my hand and I dared not let go because I'd never get him back. Jack dragged me half way down the damn street. I never made a peep. Fear and embarrassment kept me quiet. Finally, Super Jack turned back into Regular Jack.

I was alive. Blood dripped down my side. Pulling up my shirt revealed great horrors. Oh my God. I hobbled back home. From time to time, Jack looked back at me wondering why the fuck I was moving so slow. I made it home and told Camilla. She asked me why, for the love of God, I didn't just let go of Jack's leash. I told her I didn't want to lose him because Dad loved him so much. There were tears in her eyes. There were tears in mine, too, when she put the iodine all over the sidewalk-burn. I've always had this great sense of responsibility.

It's funny how old neighborhoods tell you where to go. I find myself walking up the block and down French Road. These roads lead you places like a friend from way-back with a mischievous streak. The sidewalks are contours beaten down and built up again by ancient suburban energies. In the case of Cheektowaga sidewalks, they're not that ancient because the town was founded in 1839. But that's pretty damn old for an American town. Also, unless you want to be an egocentric prick, you have to take into consideration the Seneca Indians who were here well before the white man's 1839.

You never know. Some thirty-seven-year-old brave may have walked down this same path. And perhaps he was kicked out of the longhouse by his mother. It could even be that she was near the end too. Maybe he didn't know how to come to terms with her failing health or how to best facilitate her leaving this earth or becoming one again with it or disappearing altogether or going into the sky or whatever it is that people do when they die. And that's the thing about what we call death. No one has the answer. We are sure there is an endpoint. A lot of religions suggest some aspect of a reset or even a superior reset like going to heaven as long as you haven't played with your pee pee too much or whatever. The thought of heaven actually does not do much to alleviate my anxiety. It opens the possibility to too many questions about the thereafter when the now seems pretty damn important.

I think about that brave's great grandkids and wonder if they are on one of the reservations nearby, or, if like me, they're struggling screenwriters in Los Angeles who have just returned home. Perhaps, like me, they are not really returning home, but passing through while reminiscing and stirring some of their old ghost memories. When I was a kid, I remember my father stopping on the res for gas and cigarettes because it was cheaper due to no federal or state taxes. At the time, it was the farthest I'd been from my neighborhood in Cheektowaga. The reservation was an entirely new world to me, but I was way more excited than I was scared.

The old man behind the counter had long black hair. Seeing a man with hair that length amazed me. I wished I could be part of his world; that I could grow out my hair too and work behind the counter just like him. At first, when I relayed those thoughts to my father, he was amused. Later, when I wouldn't let it go, he was annoyed. My father was always a little scared of my imagination. He didn't know where it would lead, but he anticipated it would be away from him. Dad wasn't wrong.

Despite my father's annoyance, my affinity and respect for the Seneca Nation grew through middle school and into high school. I took every opportunity to study the Senecas and to side with them whenever they were being mistreated by the white man.

Back in 1992 there was one such mistreatment and a subsequent awkward dinner conversation when I brought it up. The state was attempting to tax the Seneca's gas and cigarette sales again despite a prior treaty promising otherwise. My father and Camilla were already familiar with the situation as it was all over the Buffalo News. The Senecas on the Cattaraugus Indian Reservation fought back, and I was totally on their side. My father was not.

To show their outrage, the Senecas protested and burned tires. When the New York State Troopers came to break up the protest, they threw down tires from an overpass onto the New York State Thruway that ran through their land. The state police moved in to bust up the protest. Thirteen protesters and four troopers were hurt. Even the commander of the state troopers was hit in the head by a two-by-four.

So, I brought all this up at dinner in, admittedly, a precocious manner. My father was not amused. He shot down all my arguments with grunts and complaints that the Italians had it hard, too.

My father said something like, *But we worked hard and didn't burn tires and make the highway difficult to drive on.* I couldn't let it rest on that stupid argument. I said rather animatedly that, *cigarettes were the economic life blood to the reservations and the state wanted to get their grubby hands on a piece of that action. If, as Italians, our lands were stolen and then we were given a tiny sovereign nation in its place where we could sell wine and olive oil because that's all we had left and then the state took that, too, it would be almost the same thing. But it's not even close.* When my father waved me off with another dismissive grunt I shouted, *Haven't those motherfuckers broken enough treaties!* That's when my father cocked his hand and slapped me square in the mouth. I sat there and took it and tried not to cry. Then one sell-out tear fell but I kept staring ahead and Camilla didn't say anything nor did my father. We all sat there staring at the olive oil in the center of the table.

As a high-schooler, I wished I was there with the Indians to fight off the state's aggression. I still wish I had been there. My father never understood my soft spot for people on the margins. Now that I'm older, I also feel a little for the commander of the state troopers – maybe because he reminds me of my dad. I guess I have a soft spot for every-damned-thing when it comes down to it. My father believed you worked hard and did your duty and that was honorable. But did the commander have any doubts about the honor in doing his duty? I wonder if he was just a family man who was a cog in a corrupt institution and if he felt like he had to follow through on this police action even if he disagreed with it. That doesn't really matter though.

Ultimately, there are consequences for what we actually do and not for what we do but wish we didn't have to. To call dishonorable actions duty is an enormous gaping cop out. For this commander, his consequence was a two-by-four to the head. At least, it was an immediate consequence and I envy him that. I find that so many small decisions I've made end up having huge consequences later on. It's like getting bit by a poisonous spider on the forearm, but it doesn't hurt at the time, and the venom lays dormant for twenty years and out of the blue your arm falls straight off. I'd rather the crystal-clear immediacy of a two-by-four upside my head.

———

French Road is a four-lane road. It runs fairly straight and intersects with two major streets, Transit Road in one direction and Union Road in the other. The speed limit on French Road is only thirty-five miles an hour, but that doesn't stop some drivers-to-nowhere-ville from going over fifty. You have to watch your ass on French Road when you're walking in the winter.

If you can't get through the sidewalks because they're filled with snow, one might think, well, I'll walk along the shoulder. Except the shoulder isn't very wide even in the best conditions. When the plows have pushed the snow over after a storm, there's no shoulder at all. I knew a couple of guys who died that way. They were both good friends. After high school, one went to college while the other served in Iraq. Both made it home and hung out at a bar nearby to catch up. It was a nice night, thereafter, so they decided to walk home. The sidewalks weren't plowed so they walked on the side of the street. An SUV struck them. Death never makes any damn sense no matter the time or place, and the inevitable nature of it.

It's the train that's always coming right at us that ends up being a terrible surprise anyway.

When I was a kid, I took saxophone lessons at a music store on the corner of Borden and French Road. There's a new gas station built over the old music store. Why did I play saxophone? Because it was inevitable. The school didn't make us play an instrument, exactly. It was simply strongly recommended. For my parents, it was mandatory. My father played saxophone, so saxophone was my first choice after the drums were vetoed by my parents. Playing saxophone and going to college were the same in that both carried this inevitable momentum for me. The only difference was my father had limited experience in playing saxophone and no experience in college. My father wanted college for me like most dads around here dream of their kid playing for the Buffalo Bills. He encouraged college like it was the only available outcome for my life, so I truly thought it was.

In a way, I'm grateful for his encouragement. On the other hand, I wish someone could have explained to me that there are, in point of fact, many paths to adulthood and only one of them is attending a liberal arts college. That way, had I done everything the same, attended college, fallen in love with reading literature, become an English major, begun to write, incurred enormous school loan debt, moved to Los Angeles, made no money, and gotten a divorce, I'd have at least realized earlier I was on one path among many. I came to that conclusion eventually, which freed me up immensely, but I wish I came to that realization before I started playing saxophone, so I could have insisted on the drums.

The music store where I took saxophone lessons was called, rather artfully in its simplicity, The Music Place. The store was transplanted to the suburbs from Buffalo after its original neighborhood went "bad." Sadly, in Buffalo, that probably meant the neighborhood went black. In the seventies, you could see a caravan of white people fleeing the city every time a black family moved into their neighborhood. At least, I imagine you could see it. Fear of change does funny things to people. And being afraid of change is the absolute dumbest type of fear because change is inevitable. Holding onto the present is like trying to hold onto the ghosts of the recently departed. They're already gone and life is never going to be the same again, no matter the striving or honest grief.

That fear of the other really devastated Buffalo. When my dad died, I drove through the east side near where he grew up. It was like the entire area had been carpet-bombed. Homes had been burned out. Lots were vacant and unkempt. The only places open were liquor stores, scattered every several blocks. I remember seeing this graffiti that really spoke to me. Mind you, this was as the second Iraq War wound down. The graffiti read, "The War is Here." No kidding, right?

The man who taught my saxophone lessons was an Italian guy named Vincent Vecchiarelli. He was a true old-timer. I had only seen the likes of him at the occasional family reunion. Vincent wore wrinkled dress slacks and shirts that smelled of coffee and cigarettes. He also carried this old-world sing-song cadence in his voice when he'd get annoyed at me for playing incorrectly.

I learned by listening and repeating Vincent's every note. He played sax with dips in his notes so I played with dips. I was a little kid playing like a seventy-five-year-old man. The only problem was the contemporary jazz style had changed so I took shit for it at school. Fuck it. I'm honored I played like him. Playing like Vincent meant something once, and though change is necessary and something to be unafraid of, it's not always superior. Some things are just different stylistic choices.

Camilla told me Vincent died a few years back. It was after my father died. His heart gave out. The man had a huge heart. It played through his saxophone. I bet it dipped until the very moment it did not. That's how it was for all the old Italian saxophonists, even for my father.

I head into the Sunoco as if led there by a force greater than myself. It's like any other gas station but it's quite large. At first glance, it appears mostly filled with fluorescent lights shining down on Doritos-packed aisles. A couple of older guys in Buffalo Bills jackets meander around. They look rough so they could be anywhere between ages forty and seventy. One is glancing at a newspaper; the other peruses the beer cooler. It's ten in the morning but I don't judge, not solely on drinking in the morning. There's no one at the cash register. My cold hands beg for something warm to hold. I grab a Styrofoam cup and pour myself some coffee. It's light brown and gross but that's not the point. The heat provides welcome relief.

A sloppy-looking employee walks in through the front door and stomps the snow off his boots. Then, coming from the storage room, Priya makes her way to the counter. I head up to the register.

"Hi Tommy. I'll check you out." Priya speaks softly but she's not shy. I like that in a purely platonic asexual kind of way, given her age, of course. "Coffee, huh?"

"Yeah," I mumble.

"What you up to?"

"Just walking around."

Priya's eyes grow a little wide. She must think I'm crazy. No one normal walks outside in winter when it's this cold, even diehard Buffalonians. And she's right. I'm not normal. Writers are irregular. Speaking of writing, I probably should do some of that. I don't have a writing job right now, not that that's a surprise. The great illusion about Hollywood is people work and make a living. From time to time, you have a writing job that pays okay if you're lucky and connected. Most of the time you're writing on spec. That means you write a story and try to sell it. The market's not hot these days. It's actually colder than a bare tit in a Buffalo winter. The major studios only make about two hundred films a year. When you don't have a writing job, you're either writing a spec and/or teaching wannabe screenwriters, the poor saps.

I simply cannot write another script that never sells; that never gets made into a movie. Even if no one else ever reads it, I want to write something just for me.

Here's the pitch on the novel.

My book's about a man who believes he's turning into a wolf. It is in no way about me.

"I'm heading home. Want to walk back with me?" Priya asks.

"Of course."

I'm flattered she trusts me to walk her home. She doesn't know me really. But she knows my mom and that's good enough for her, I think. I plan on taking this responsibility seriously. Women, and especially young women, have to protect themselves more than men. It's an undeniable fact of both nature and society. And when a woman decides you're someone she doesn't have to worry about as a threat in this fucked up world, that's something to honor.

Priya and I plod back up French Road toward home. I imagine we are explorers in a distant land, but then I see we are stepping in the same tracks I made en route to the gas station. Priya and I are talking about high school.

"I don't like going at all. In fact, it's terrible. There are so many awful things about it. I don't even know where to start." Priya talks quite a bit and faster than I expected, and in a higher voice than I imagined.

"I never did either," I tell her when she takes a breath. Her home, like my childhood home, is actually in South Cheektowaga, but the school district boundaries don't line up perfectly with the town's. So Priya, like I did many years ago, goes to West Seneca East Senior High School in the town of West Seneca, even though her residency is in Cheektowaga.

"All my friends in the neighborhood go to school in Cheektowaga," she explains. "The Cheektowaga school kids mostly hang together and the West Seneca kids do, too. So, I'm always caught in the middle."

"I get it. It was the same way when I was in school."

"How old are you?"

"I'm old. Like super old." Priya doesn't laugh at my sense of humor and that doesn't bruise my ego too much.

"If I had a car, that would be so cool. Everything would be so much better. I could hang out with my school friends whenever I want."

Somehow, I turn into my father, "At least you don't have to pay for gas."

"What kind of car do you have?"

"A BMW."

"Cool. What type?"

"An old sedan for an old man like me."

Priya seems a bit disappointed.

"It's a convertible," I offer up.

"Oh, that's cool."

I don't blame Priya much for her attitude about high school and other things. High school was terrible. The god-awful uniformity of it. All the lockers looked the same – metal, almost-tan and equidistant. And their insides weren't that different. Each of them filled with social studies books that stunk of half-told truths sold to us suburbanites by monolithic corporate publishing houses. And then there was the actual smell of stale lunches – the bouquet of week-old peanut butter and jelly with the occasional tuna fish or egg salad thrown in for pungent measure. The selfsame walls were there to keep out more than radical thought. The thick off-white concrete never hid its true intent to keep students in and any real semblance of actual culture out. And the people in high school all looked the same.

There were the same old clowns in different colored suits: jocks, preps, punk rockers, slackers, smokers, druggies, the straight edge crew, choral nerds, orchestra geeks, band freaks, guys with long leather trench coats, AP Kids, the cool teacher, the drill sergeant teacher, the nice vice principal, the totalitarian principal, etc. If you were good looking you were pretty okay and you were able to operate more freely among the wobbly alliances of imbeciles. Good-looking kids had a little agency. Enjoy it while you can, kiddos. But if you weren't an eight, nine, or ten out of ten in looks, you were naked out there and desperate to find a social uniform that could keep you protected from the jackals.

At the same time, there was occasional beauty in the asylum. A musical note played truly by the one kid in the band who was really good, or a painting rendered by the local malcontent hung up proudly by the pot smoking art teacher. I remember being a freshman with a locker next to a bunch of senior girls. Several of them were very beautiful to me, but one in particular. I liked her face. It was milky white and pleasant, and her hair was brunette and long. She never wore much makeup because she didn't need to. Once, she bent over in front of me at her locker and her ass was so perfect some part of me jumped on the inside. I think it was my heart. This little story tells a lot about men, and not just teenagers. Our hearts can actually do flips when we see an immaculately sculpted ass. This story also says something about beauty. It's everywhere, and when you truly see it, it can grab your heart and give it a good twist. I wonder what that hot senior is doing now. Is she a pleasant-faced mom with two cherubic-looking kids, or has life beaten the beauty out of her?

Right there, on a patch of ice, I make a vow to never look at

Priya's behind on purpose. At that very moment, Priya jaunts ahead of me to walk in my old footsteps. A long coat covers her backside. I am very grateful. The long coat makes me almost feel I'm not noticing the curves of her buttocks at all.

We've made it back to Crabapple Court. My house is on the way to Priya's. She stares at the haphazard tracks all over the front yard.

"What the heck did that?" she asks.

"I don't know.

"Could it be a bunch of deers?"

Should I correct her? If I do, that may come off as rude. She might be testing me though. "You mean deer?"

"Isn't it deers when plural?"

She seems convinced its deers. Am I wrong? Stick with your instincts. "No, it's deer."

"Huh. They must have been hungry," she says staring at the gnaw marks on the crabapple tree.

"They must be looking for food farther from the woods than usual."

"Those deer seem angry or something."

She's using deer now. That's a relief. "Why would you say that?"

"They, like, ripped up your mom's whole front yard."

Priya has a point. The tracks are oddly shaped and aggressive. They seem larger than deer. Much bigger. And not really hooves but paws. It appears more likely there were several pawed-animals who made these prints, but the tracks have been trampled over and over again to such an extent it's difficult to tell if there was one animal or many.

The tracks remind me of those my childhood dog, Jack, might have made. He used to get so excited before bedtime. I'd let him out in the back yard and he would do frantic laps around the above-ground pool until he tired himself out. During those spells, Jack was feral like a wolf in the wild. After he tired himself out, he'd jaunt up to me and cock his head. Jack would want me to pet him and to really look in his eyes. He wanted me to understand the wildness was gone and the affable dog I knew had returned.

My leg still hurts from last night. I wonder why I just lied to Priya about the deer. These tracks are not cervine. My stomach is hurting. I guess I didn't really lie. An oversimplification is more accurate. There's a very thin line between oversimplifying and out and out telling a lie.

I have this moral impulse to always be honest. When I know I've been dishonest, I physically hurt. The pain strikes me right in my core – in my gut and I get queasy. I figure it's some sort of evolutionary adaptation that was useful thousands of years ago, but is not at all helpful in the current age where lying is the contemporary currency. Imagine being in a corporate meeting doubled over in pain because of the daily lies one hands out like breath mints. Perhaps thousands of years ago being honest helped with human survival. Like, back then, saying what you meant with certainty and truth and believing it really mattered. For instance, "There's a saber-tooth. Run, motherfucker!"

If and when there's a pharmaceutical zombie apocalypse, I suppose my obsolete honesty adaptation may again become useful. And you know in your gut that's how the apocalypse will happen, pharmaceutically induced. In areas like Buffalo where the economy's been terrible for thirty years, psychiatrists hand out psychotropic medications more vociferously than crack pushers.

The typical pharmaceutical business model is to mass market a bad pill so that a new good pill can be offered up to fix the bad pill's effects. Some genius pharmaceutical sales rep is finally going to convince their higher-ups to give us a really bad pill, underlining the belief that this strategy will equal sales straight through the fucking roof. But the good pill won't be enough to counteract the

Armageddon-pill and, presto wacko, we'll have a pharmaceutical zombie apocalypse.

Speaking of survival skills for the apocalypse, I used to practically live in the woods across the way when I was a kid. This one neighborhood teen, Kyle, thought he was a commando or something. At first, he seemed cool because he was all into the wilderness and knew a bunch of survival skills. The truth is he was a private school brat with some anger issues. He was also pretty good-looking and charismatic, too. My best guess is he's now a very effective cult leader.

Kyle had a club he ran out in the woods. I was six years younger than him. He liked me probably because I was also good-looking and charismatic. Kyle asked me if I wanted into the club so I said sure. There was an initiation due to the secret nature of his organization. I was weirded out even though I was like eight years old, but he assured me nothing ill would come of me. So, he initiated me into the club. My initiation was entirely painless. He said the words, "You're in," spit in his hand, and shook mine. And that was that. I was in.

There was another kid Kyle's age named Joey who wanted into the club, too. I think he was, like Kyle, also a Catholic school kid. But Joey was less of a prick than Kyle. His one great flaw was he wanted to fit in. Kyle really put Joey through it. He was blindfolded, tripped, and embarrassed. I was just supposed to watch, but I became increasingly uncomfortable. At one point, I pleaded with Kyle to stop. After what felt like an eternity, Kyle must've gotten bored. He took off Joey's blindfold and reluctantly let him in the club. But even though I was much younger, I was in the club more than Joey ever would be. And, when it came down to it, I didn't give two shits about the club. Even then, I suspected the entire thing was bullshit. I didn't know the word for Kyle's behavior back then. But it was power and it was mean and it was gross. I vowed to myself that I would never be like Kyle. Spending time in the woods diminished thereafter.

Priya talks about the animal tracks as my mind wanders from my childhood dog Jack, to the pharmaceutical zombie apocalypse, to the woods. As soon as she stops for a breath I interject. "There used to be wild turkeys in those woods when I was a kid." Just like that, I change the subject from freaky, mysterious animal tracks to the woods and wild turkeys. It's a funny thing. I hate dishonesty, yet I can change the subject as easily as I pass gas. If you were to interview my ex-wife, and I don't recommend it given she has darts for fingers and loves shaking sensitive appendages, she can attest to the high flatulence standards I hold for myself. Mainly, my ability to fart on command and even, on occasion, incorporate ass-shaking dance routines alongside my staccato trumpet-toots and tuba, earthquake blasts.

I hate dishonesty, yet I live in Los Angeles and write for Hollywood whenever God smirks at me. That's kinda like hating coconut cream pie but trying one's best to consume coconut cream pie at every possible opportunity. It's so damn easy for me to avoid the truth and make up stories. In fact, it's the thing I'm really great at. Telling stories is lying and don't let any storyteller tell you otherwise. I'm unsure if my paradoxical existence is true for everyone as a pivotal piece of the human condition or if I am utterly alone in this grand cluster-fuck delusion – one person on one planet among a world of planets among a world of universes shaking his fist at the expanse of everything/nothing and hating the religion of dishonesty but being one of its most dutiful practitioners.

I've bored Priya sufficiently with my stories about wild turkeys. Her disinterest is fine because I am one-thousand percent platonic about our budding friendship, mentorship, acquaintanceship. As Priya and I are saying our goodbyes, we see Sal's truck pull into her driveway.

For a moment, I'm embarrassed to be with Priya due to either her young age or my old age, and I feel a sharp pain in my stomach. I don't think Sal can see us clearly through the crabapple tree that's partially obscuring all of our views. At first, I'm grateful for that. In any case, Sal seems distracted and on some sort of mission. He steps out of his truck and leaves the door wide open. I guess that's his thing. Pop-country-western music blares from inside. This makes no sense. I thought he was one of those wannabe hard rockers or whatever. Sal moves to the truck bed and unloads a stack of newspapers. He takes the papers and puts them into a large wooden, blue newspaper box at the end of the driveway.

"What's Sal doing?" I mutter. "He's a newspaper boy?"

"No. My brother is... Neel. Sal supervises all the delivery boys."

Priya and I watch as Neel exits the house wearing a muscle shirt and a beanie. Sal and Neel bump fists and exchange money. Now the crabapple tree is a pain in the ass. It's unclear, but it looks like Neel is handing over a lot of money. Sal takes the time to count it out. My gut says this is weird.

"My brother's crazy," Priya says as she strolls to her house.

"So is my cousin," I direct to her backside.

Priya doesn't look back and I'm grateful for that. I absolutely cannot and will not fall in love with a teenager. Sal pulls out of the driveway and fishtails as he speeds off. I take a mental note to figure out what the fuck is going on with Sal and Neel. I watch Priya as she walks up her driveway and enters her house.

It's possible Sal's delivery boy supervision is a part-time job he's a bit embarrassed about and that's why he hasn't mentioned it. But delivering papers doesn't seem like Sal. The thing is, I'm not really sure who Sal is anymore. I'm starting to realize that's true for a lot of people who I thought I really knew. My ex-wife was someone I understood and then not. It was like that with my ex-girlfriend. I knew her until I didn't, as well. Camilla's been surprising me since I've come home. She's softer than I remember, and more in tune with the suffering of others. Now, Sal is either a humbled worker-bee for the Buffalo News or he's doing something nefarious. Most of all, I can't trust myself anymore. Something dark is growing inside me. But I don't think it's dark as in evil, but dark as in old and primal. I bend over and put my hand in the tracks. My cold hand looks more like a paw. I barely recognize myself these days.

SIX

ROUTINE ADVENTURES

I'm ever fascinated by the routine misadventures of the miraculously mundane. It's been two weeks since I made my grand return to Buffalo, home of the Buffalo Bills, my dying mother, and the new terrain for an ancient awakening wolf-like animal.

Though I always set my alarm for eight, I wake up at seven in the morning. When I wake, my heart beats rapidly – sometimes it's on the snare and other times the bass drum. Often, I wake up sore like I've run a marathon in my sleep. I never think of Priya. Rather, I never think of Priya sexually. She's often on my mind but I rarely see her. Camilla's sent me on errands to the gas station a couple of times. Priya and I talk and I'm haunted by her innocence. It reminds me of something I feel I've lost and can never get back. I never linger long when we chat. She asks about Camilla. I sigh and ask about Neel. She rolls her eyes. Priya says hello. I say goodbye. She also wears Beatles shirts but has never listened to their music. I think that's sad, but I don't say anything in order to avoid shaming her.

Neel delivers the morning paper before heading to school, so I see him daily. Camilla will not allow me to make us breakfast despite adamant protestations. She has agreed, however, to let me retrieve the paper from the front lawn wherever Neel has chucked it. Being Priya's brother seems to be Neel's most redeemable quality, because he sure is not a great newspaper delivery boy. He's rarely on time and he has terrible aim. Neel chucks the paper from the sidewalk because he's too lazy to walk up the driveway.

Neel's newspaper throwing is not because the driveway is filled with snow. Camilla has allowed me to shovel the driveway, so I do it religiously each day like my father did after he retired. And I feel retired. I have no paid writing job right now. My "manager" won't return my calls. Fuck him. So, I write my novel as I'm able and I shovel and I gather the newspaper.

In the morning, I wait at the window while breakfast is being made until I see Neel coming. I watch him hurl the paper. The curious thing is how excited I become in anticipation of the paper and the pleasure I get retrieving it and giving it to Camilla. At breakfast, she divides the paper between us. I am allotted the sports and the front page. Camilla gets the local news, the arts and entertainment, and the religion sections. The religion section is her primary read lately. It gives her some comfort, she says. That portion of the paper doesn't provide me any.

I've been more interested in the local news these days, particularly the police blotter. After Camilla's done with the local section, I pour over it expecting to see Sal's name there. It hasn't happened yet. Sal hasn't called or stopped by since the party. I'm sure he's busy with grand misadventures of his own. Camilla says I should look in on his mother, Audrey, if I want to get a hold of him. Mom and Audrey don't speak very much. It has something to do with a past grievance Camilla refuses to talk about. It's an Italian thing. That really means, it's a shepherding thing.

My ancestors were Sicilian shepherds on both sides of my family going back generations. Shepherds never forget a grudge. If you kill one of their sheep, they'll kill two of yours. If you kill two sheep, they'll kill one of your children. It's not because they are particularly vengeful. It's because the flock is the lifeblood of their family. If you mess with the lifeblood, then you need to know the boundary and they will let you know where that line is in the starkest terms possible. I think I'll pay Audrey a visit.

After breakfast, I write the novel for a couple of hours, or at least I try to. I write by the window and look out at the crabapple tree. There are tracks out there most days. Camilla sits at a corner chair and reads romantic novels that have bare-chested men on the covers.

When I was young, I could not write if Camilla was in the room. She always wanted to be a part of everything. She was forever right over my shoulder staring down at my work. Never in judgment. She just wanted to be writing with me, too. Back then, the writing had to be mine and only mine. I'd freeze up if she was behind me and I could feel the anger rising up my back. Sometimes I'd snap at her, and often I'd feel guilty after. Now, I can only write in this house if Camilla is in the same room with me.

Mom likes to listen, so I read her portions of the novel. It's called "I Animal." The book's kind of changing a little from what I originally intended. With writing, that tends to happen. You plot your course and then the winds fuck up the itinerary. The novel's now more about a man who begins to fear he's turning into a wolf after he learns his best friend is dying. It still has absolutely nothing to do with my particular circumstance, so don't get that twisted. Camilla laughs a lot at what I read to her. It gives me great pleasure. Sadly, the novel's not really intended to be comedic. Hearing her big laugh is worth any embarrassment on my part. I tell her it's not supposed to be funny.

She always reminds me, "What do you know? You're only the writer." My mother missed her calling. She should've been a Hollywood producer.

SEVEN

REACQUAINTANCE

Camilla let me take her car to Audrey's. It's a Saturn station wagon. They don't make Saturns anymore, and for good reason. Personally, I never understood the brand. Saturn cars are by no measure futuristic. They aren't sleek. They aren't technologically advanced. They are just, serviceable. I'm not interested in merely serviceable whether we are discussing cars or blowjobs. My father, Frank, was very proud of his Saturn. This station wagon is one of two he originally bought brand new at the same time. People in the neighborhood thought he was crazy. They considered it impractical to buy two new cars at once. The neighbors were also suspicious of any brand of car other than Ford. Lower-middle class people are obsessed with routine like Hollywood types are with their own asses. Why couldn't Frank just buy a Ford like everyone else? Frank refused to buy Fords.

Dad's father had worked for Ford and was laid off when Frank was a kid. Grandpa never really recovered from the layoff. He had always been a drinker and the layoff was the last excuse he needed to never come out of the bottle again. Frank, like Camilla, could keep a grudge. Also, Frank appreciated Saturn dealerships were haggle-free. In other words, the price on the car was the price you paid. My father had a very low tolerance for bullshit. I've half-inherited the trait. The bullshit of others really bothers me, but I'm a very strong swimmer swimming in a vat of my own reeking bullshit.

Audrey's place is in Depew, a village adjacent Cheektowaga. Where Cheektowaga is a cultural wasteland, Depew's an industrial wasteland, and that's before all the industry closed down. Its motto is "The Village of Unexcelled Opportunity." Depew stinks. At least, that's the way I remember it as a kid. It always smelled to me like a factory of ass. The village had some industry when I was a kid built around the railroad that runs through it.

Big Sal worked at a factory that built railway car parts and couplings. Some workers there ended up with Mesothelioma cancer on account of asbestos exposure. Big Sal was one of them. Depew also had a lot of bars back then. It still does. Depew is a hard place, sad on its best days with quiet streets filled only with the simmering tension of unfulfilled opportunities. This is the cauldron I mostly dodged, and Little Sal was steeped in from birth. Depew makes Cheektowaga look cosmopolitan. Little Sal always found a way to get to my neighborhood when we were kids so we could play together. He was a persistent child. I'll give him that. Audrey finally kicked Big Sal out of the house when Little Sal was ten years old. She had caught him cheating on her again. Little Sal looked for any excuse to get away from the troubles back home.

Camilla and Audrey used to be great friends when each of them was first married. My father used to look in on Little Sal and Audrey from time to time, even when Big Sal was still around the house. My father knew Big Sal could not be relied on for matrimonial or fatherly duties. You have to remember Frank and Big Sal were first cousins who grew up in the same neighborhood in Cheektowaga, near Delavan Avenue. That phrasing, "you have to remember," is from my father. He always said to people, "you have to remember." The expression was super annoying to me. Now, look at me. I'm doing the same damned thing. My father was trying to say, "I want you to really hear me," but it came out as, "you have to remember." Nonetheless, it may be important to remember but it's far more important not to repeat past mistakes.

Audrey and my mother grew up near Delavan, too. The area of Cheektowaga they all came up in was practically Buffalo. Point of fact, it was right on the edge of the city. My understanding is Big Sal was the petty hoodlum in the old neighborhood on Delavan. He was a small man but liked to act very big. In that, his girth suited his act. Apparently, the petty crime slowed when he was older. But one time when I was over there playing with Little Sal, we saw a bunch of boxes of paper towels he stole from the factory. Even then, it seemed like an odd thing to steal. We were told by Big Sal to keep our mouths shut.

The man acted big everywhere except where he was needed most. Even though Big Sal and my father had moved from their old neighborhood, my father was the one to move upward, however slightly. Our place in South Cheektowaga was decidedly more suburban than Big Sal's place in Depew. It's almost as if Big Sal slipped a bit by moving from the old neighborhood, because at least the neighborhood on Delavan had a sense of history. At best, Big Sal made a parallel move. Both were dying neighborhoods whose more industrious days had long since passed.

Somehow, my father owned Big Sal's shortcomings, because he had Catholic guilt. And my father could not abide by that, given he believed we could do good to make up for our sins. My father always tried to fill in some of the gaps for Audrey and Sal. Naturally, the frequency of Frank's visits picked up when Audrey finally gave Big Sal the boot. There was man's work around the house and Frank tried to spend extra time with Little Sal. Then Big Sal died about six months later. He hadn't told anyone about his cancer until the very end. Frank's responsibilities to Audrey and Little Sal only increased. For about a year, my father was practically living at both homes on account of how much work he had to do to keep both households afloat.

Suddenly, my father stopped going to help out Audrey and Little Sal. I didn't mind because I was able to see my father more. Like most kids, I was a little selfish and didn't really like having to share my father with Little Sal. Unbeknownst to me at the time, Frank had received his orders from his boss over at Crabapple Court to stop seeing Audrey and Sal. You see, Camilla suspected Frank of having an affair with Audrey. She had no proof, mind you. Just her gut; and Camilla comes from a family line with very weak stomachs.

I was there when Camilla confronted Audrey. She invited Audrey to the house to play cards. Thankfully, Audrey didn't bring Little Sal. Camilla ambushed Audrey and Frank during a game of euchre. I saw the whole thing from the top of the stairs. None of them knew I was there. There were denials. There was crying. There were angry words between Audrey, Frank, and Camilla. Bad blood has been present between Audrey and Camilla ever since. Audrey never remarried. She also never forgave my mother for the suggestion she and Frank did anything untoward.

For my part, I believed, and continue to believe my father was innocent of the affair. But I never resented Camilla for what she did because I had my father's full attention back. I saw Little Sal less and less after the ambush. Back then I didn't really care about Little Sal's feelings, but I wonder how he feels about all this now. What does he think really happened between our families? For about a year or so, we shared my father like brothers. Afterward, Frank was all mine, for better or worse. Sal and I were pretty good friends when we were little. After the ambush, we were more like acquaintances. There were still occasions to see each other once in a while, but the rift between our mothers affected us, too. Neither of us really trusted each other thereafter. We remained mirrors of ourselves, but distant mirrors. I suspect that's not changed.

After Frank died, Camilla and Audrey began speaking a little again. Camilla says she was the first to call. Audrey claims it's the other way around. The truth is the funeral brought them back together and tensions slightly thawed. There's nothing like grieving to get Italians back on speaking terms.

I've reached Audrey's house on Muskegon Road. The houses are much closer together than on Crabapple Court. People practically live on top of each other over here. Maybe that's because almost all the homes on this street are double-deckers. Audrey lives in the first-floor unit of her double-decker. She was able to buy it with the settlement money she finally received from the company five years after Big Sal's death. At least she received something from the corporation that killed her fat, philandering husband. The suits decided Sal's entire life was only worth forty-five thousand dollars. Maybe that explains a lot about Sal's degenerate behavior. If a man's life is valued so little, how can he be expected to have any sense as to how to value himself or those he loves?

Audrey kisses my cheek and ushers me into her house graciously like a queen from Depew might. She wears a long garment I've only ever seen Italian grandmothers wear. Italian women of that age buy these dresses in the plus-sized section at department stores like Kmart. The gown's purple and has a floral pattern on its very bottom edge. I can tell Audrey's ankles are swollen with water.

After Big Sal died, Audrey took up drinking booze. She sometimes will still refer to Big Sal as her husband because they never officially divorced before he passed on. The truth is they would have never divorced no matter how long he lived, on a matter of principal because they were Catholic. In a way, I admire that sort of resolve, sticking some institution out when it's utterly absurd, devoid of all prior meaning, and, in fact, likely detrimental to mental health by that point. That kind of resolve reminds me a great deal of my marriage to writing. When Audrey finally gave up boozing a few years back, she began drinking water in its place. Unfortunately, she drinks so much water her entire body swells up.

"Would you like some water, dear?" Audrey asks.

I'm horrified. Not only because I have the suspicion Audrey's organs are swimming in excess water, but because she pours herself a glass from the tap. I never drink tap water. Foo-foo bottled water is my thing. You have to remember, I'm Los Angeles now, baby. I also never drink tap water in Depew, in particular. There might be carcinogens in the water from the old factory.

Even though Little Sal and I are second cousins, I always refer to Audrey as my aunt. "No thanks, Aunt Audrey. You're looking good."

Aunt Audrey pours me a glass of tap water anyway and places it in front of me at the kitchen table.

"I'm not. You were always a flatterer. Never had a problem with getting girls like my Sal did."

Sal never married. Truly, I don't remember Sal ever having a girlfriend. I never found this weird. Growing up, it was just a matter of fact. Sal has always been the kind of guy girls don't like. He just didn't have that "it" factor. And whatever he did have implied a needy void no woman dared to fill.

Audrey's right about me, though. I've never had a problem attracting women. Picking the wrong ones and getting rid of them upon discovering their failings are separate issues. I think women like me on account of my relative good looks and the general distant-quality that seeps out of my existential being. Tall, dark, and distant is catnip to lots of women. It seems to me if you're partially detached from an incomprehensible, inescapable tragic reality, it's quite easy to get a woman interested. Women have, historically, always wanted to draw me back from my distant fantasy-world toward the near-sighted abyss of reality. I've pretended to let some of them because I found them attractive or didn't want to be alone. Sometimes I even convinced myself I could save them or they could save me. In special circumstances I even tried to love them more than myself and that destroyed us more spectacularly than anything. Or maybe I'm just an asshole.

"What went wrong between you and Mom?

I already know the answer, but I still feel compelled to ask Aunt Audrey her side of the story by a force some people say is God, and I don't know for sure but I do know it comes from deep within. For me, it's usually positioned in my weak stomach. And it burns. It always burns. Some people don't have the burning. Those are the people to avoid because they lack enough instinct to keep themselves and anyone in close proximity alive. Not only does this sort of person never turn the wheel, they never even see the car coming before the crash.

Aunt Audrey cocks her head sideways for what feels like forever. I can only imagine she is thinking deeply and this is her rarely used posture for that activity. Against my better judgment, I take a sip of water rather than run out of the room screaming to break the tension.

"I loved your father."

I practically spit the water out of my mouth. Then I overcompensate and suck it back down too fast. I'm choking and not the no-big-deal one-second choke. This is the kind of choke if you're by yourself you're slamming your torso into the end of a table. But I am not by myself, and Aunt Audrey was a cafeteria monitor in her heyday. I don't know if that's where she learned this strategy or not but she's waving her hands like airport ground crew and screaming at me in a manly voice, "Cough it out! Cough it out, baby!"

Aunt Audrey's fucking terrifying, so I swing my head backward to get away. Along with my head follows the rest of my body and I tip my chair backwards. I crash to the floor and squirm on my side like a fish out of water. Audrey can't really bend over so she's standing over me and wildly pummels me with her fists on my kidneys. I had no idea the woman could hit that hard. Still choking, I manage to get up. My arms are flailing as I plead for her not to hit me. When she won't desist, I take off running around the table to escape the beating.

"Cough it up, baby!" she screams.

Aunt Audrey chases me around the table and pins me against a chair. She keeps smacking me until I finally stop choking. At this point I'm sprawled over the table and my arms are outstretched like Christ, and the air feels better than ever before. I really thought that was it for me. It's a funny thing. Sure, I was a little afraid, but mostly I was just surprised. As in, this is how I'm going out? Maybe I'd have given into temptation at the thought of peace thereafter but Aunt Audrey was so damn persistent. Italian, former cafeteria monitors are resolute people I guess.

"I loved your father and I loved your mother, too," Audrey says. "Nothing ever went on between me and Frank. You remind me of him, you know?"

In that moment, Aunt Audrey becomes beautiful again like she was so many years ago and I start thinking of my father sitting at this table having dinner with his other family. Aunt Audrey is fawning over him and not in some perverse way. He just fixed the kitchen sink because it had been leaking. She's giving him a beer to thank him. He finishes it quickly out of politeness, stands, and heads for the door.

Audrey grabs me by the shoulders. "I don't blame Camilla anymore. She loved your father. She's a good person. She's just always had a hard time believing in the goodness of other people."

Damn, when did Aunt Audrey get so smart? I believe every word she's saying and it rattles me. If Camilla has been so wrong, what am I missing in my own life? Where is my blind spot? I know enough to know the punch you don't see coming is the one that knocks you straight out. My marriage was like that. That fleshy little assassin with crab claws for hands hit me with a two-by-four to the back of the head while I was tying my shoes at the church of our relationship. What else am I missing?

"I need to talk to Sal, Aunt Audrey."

"Try the French Lounge."

The French Lounge is neither French nor a lounge. It's more of a family diner. They do serve French onion soup and French Fries, however. That's as French as it gets in Buffalo. Truth be told, it's called the French Lounge because it's on French Road. I don't blame the ownership for trying a little too hard to sell their product. I'm a screenwriter. My lot will say or do anything to make a sale. "Split Pea Alien Family Soup" was a screenplay I shopped around. It was as its name suggests, about a family of aliens who made split pea soup to fit into their community in Moscow, Idaho. I threw in a bunch of throw-back jokes about the Soviets because Soviets were funny a few years back. After a series of shenanigans and near misses, the alien family takes first prize in the county fair's soup competition. I shit you not, it killed in meetings. Money is money.

I grab a seat at a booth where I can see the front door. Either Westerns taught me that or it's an evolutionary type-thing. Keeping my back to the wall and facing the door is a real personal priority. Despite my Western attitude, I've only fired a BB gun once. My buddy in college had one and I shot it at a glass coke bottle two times. I missed on both occasions. Liking shooting the gun was expected. But I didn't, and gave it back to him as soon as possible. If I wanted to destroy something, I always felt it was easier and more intimate to use my hands. Destruction from a distance never appealed.

An actual fight has eluded me my whole life. Sure, I was in a couple of youthful soccer scrums but that's all pushing and shoving. That doesn't mean I wouldn't get in a fight should the opportunity arise. I'm ready, always. As usual, the first thing I do after I sit down is assess potential threats, and then develop a physical response scheme to minimize them to greatest effect if the potential threats become actual problems. I know no women to admit to doing this activity. Almost every dude I've ever talked to about this behavior has been right on board. Like, "Man, I'm so glad you mentioned that. I don't feel alone anymore."

Men are fairly stupid animals. We're like dogs but dumber, and less loyal. We're animals that aren't particularly good at violence, but we are excellent at mentally preparing to protect ourselves – should the opportunity arise. If men actually did their jobs rather than preparing for possible aggression against us at restaurants, this world would be filled with more bridges and art and much less flatulence. That said, you can't take this away from us. Sizing up possible foes and scheming to neutralize them is the most relational thing most of us men do. When I size up a group of other men and decide which one I'd throat-punch first if they all attacked me at once, it's almost like making new friends.

There appears to be all locals in this joint. I can tell on account of how little verbal communication is going on. Most of the customer orders consist of knowing eye movements and the occasional overt nod. I wish I had that familiarity with a place of my own back in LA. Some restaurants are okay there, but it's not the same. My favorite LA restaurant is Cafe Gratitude. It's really a small chain based in California. That place is like going to a new age church of foofy veganism. As much as I detest authoritarian religions, the food is delicious.

At Cafe Gratitude you order each meal by saying "I am" and

then some sort of affirmation. As in "I am Joyful" or "I am Extraordinary." "I am Extraordinary" is a vegan BLT. It is extraordinary, and as much as I feel I should detest Cafe Gratitude, I feel content there. I think it's because the waiters and waitresses all seem like true believers. Real believers are admirable but I can never be one. It's kind of like admiring the architecture of churches or the community of cults but knowing better to enter or join.

The waiters will stare straight in your eyes and deliver their pseudo-spiritual "question of the day." Why? Because they are one-hundred-percent sincere. The question of the day is a question they put to you before you're served your meal. "What makes your heart move today?" is the question my Cafe Gratitude waitress asked me most recently. The waiters and waitresses ask the question, but it's cool and they don't expect you to answer it or anything. The questions are just food for thought, you know what I mean? I didn't know the answer to the heart question and it bothered me. Was my heart empty? No. It is not. Is it moved? It's moved. I just don't know how to describe what moves my heart in clear terms nor do I have anyone I trust fully enough to take the time to stumble around trying to sincerely find that answer. Thinking about this is distracting me. I'm not paying attention to threat assessment. And that's the time you should be paying attention the most.

A group of people walk past my table to their own. First is a big guy in a John Deer hat and a camouflage hunting jacket. The next is a plump woman holding a baby in a carrier like she's holding a bowling ball in a bag. She's wearing a scarf and it's blocking half her face. Last is a woman in a long green coat. Even with the coat I notice the shape of her body. She has a nice figure. We look at each other's eyes at the same time and she looks familiar but I can't place her.

She's finally passed me and I take a deep breath. It seems I've escaped my momentary lapse of inattentiveness unscathed. Then I hear her voice from behind. "Tommy. Tommy D'Angelo. Is that you?"

"I think so."

And then there's a long pause as I try to figure out who this person is. She takes off her winter hat to assist me. Her short brown hair suits her. I still have no clue, however.

"I'm Lauren. Lauren Townsend. Kelly's sister. You were in the same grade. I was a couple back."

As soon as she said Townsend, recognition and regret wash over me. Her sister Kelly went to my high school. She liked me when we were in eighth grade. We weren't friends or anything. Her friends told me she liked me at the fall homecoming. She wanted to slow dance. My concern was that dancing with Kelly might lead to dating or maybe marriage. I remember her friends badgering me. No amount of public pressure could make me dance with her. I was always a stubborn asshole, and my default was to dig in when pressured. A girl named Sara who I thought was cute then asked me to dance politely, and I said yes. It turned out Sara was Kelly's enemy. I heard Kelly cried when she learned I danced with her nemesis. Sara was thrilled. She was a little bitch really. I felt bad. The entire episode made me queasy. I felt manipulated by forces beyond my control. Being true to myself led to hurting someone else. I've tried to erase this juvenile episode from my mind but every so often it rises back to the surface and I beat myself up about it.

"That's right. Good to see you, Lauren."

"Are you eating by yourself?"

I look at the empty space around me a little sheepishly.

"I'm waiting on my cousin," I say. "In town for a few days. My mother's not well."

"I'm sorry to hear that. Kelly would be thrilled to say hello."

I realize Lauren is looking past me and over my shoulder to the right. I slowly turn around and see the woman from before who has now removed her scarf. She's staring straight at me. It's Kelly. She waves excitedly and I wave back. Her husband looks pissed off.

"Come over for a minute, until your cousin gets here," Lauren says.

Getting out of this is not possible. I slide out of my seat slowly. It looks like Kelly and I are going to dance after all.

"We're all real proud of you, Tommy. Living your dreams and all, writing in Los Angeles," Lauren says as Kelly shyly smiles and dotes over her cooing baby, Michael. Kelly looks pretty good, sort of. What I mean to convey is she looks happy as a mom. It suits her. She's a bit bigger-boned, but the weight's settled in her cheeks, and when she smiles she looks a lot like her baby.

Kelly's husband, Brian, is giving me the evil eye. What did I ever do to this guy? Maybe it's because he thinks I escaped from Buffalo and am living what he imagines is a life of sunny skies and beach babes he never dared to dream for himself. If that's the reason he's so mad at me, boy is he ever wrong. I never got away. Crabapple Court came with me all the way to Los Angeles. All the way running down the Venice Beach Boardwalk I carried that damn street. Sometimes I wore the stinking albatross of Crabapple Court, of Cheektowaga, of Buffalo, as a badge of honor. Other times it weighed me down as I trudged out to sea and I was sinking, baby, right to the bottom of the Pacific.

LA people are on a constant trip from their assholes to their navels to their assholes, etcetera forever. That's the reason for their general fixation on their behinds, and the behinds of others around their vicinity. But no amount of reasonably sculpted jiggling volleyball playing asses could ever give me some relief from Crabapple Court. Believe me, I've tried. I've looked for solutions in every tight ass in Los Angeles and none of them provided any real solace from the lake effect snowstorm raging inside me.

The baby fusses. For a second, I take it personally, thinking, like, really, the baby has something against me, too.

"There, there, Michael Thomas," Kelly sooths as she lovingly picks the baby up and pats his back so he can relieve the gas pressuring his nascent tummy. For a moment, I look down at my own belly and dare to wish someone would pat my back because I'm feeling gaseous, too, and then I look up to find Kelly gaping at me a little embarrassed. Holy shit, all my worst/best fears/hopes are coming true. This is all about me. Brian hates my guts not because I escaped and he didn't, but because to his wife he's always been second fiddle to this boy named Thomas (that's me) that made her cry (even though he didn't mean it and is real guilty about it in the Catholic sense, and by that I mean universally) at the eighth-grade fall dance.

My throat feels tight and my mouth dry. Fight or flight has kicked in. I think you can learn a lot about someone concerning their very first instinctual impulse when threatened. First, I feel my mouth curling and my teeth turning into what I imagine are fangs. I'm about to let everyone at the table know to back the fuck off or there will be consequences. Then, suddenly, I have the urge to flee. My body is telling me not to be brave. Run motherfucker, run, I hear coming from some dark fold of my brain.

Running is the better survival strategy. I can't fight an entire family, including a baby. There's no honor in that. And besides, I kinda like the baby. I mean, I'm happy that I didn't produce him but I'm even happier he exists and his middle name is the same as my first name. Frankly, this middle-name-sake baby is the closest thing I've ever had to a progeny of my own. It's not that I never wanted kids or, in the least, wasn't open to the possibility. The reality was my ex-wife had the maternal instincts of a drunk tube of lipstick with scissor-hands running around the house begging for hugs from everybody.

I stretch out my right leg so I can make one smooth move and a quick burst out of the booth. As I do so, I bump Lauren's foot with my leg and she smiles. It's not creepy or trying-too-hard, but one of those calming everything is going to be okay expressions because the universe is all interconnected in its disconnected chaos. I like her teeth. They aren't perfect, but they're not fangs either like mine can be. Some of the tension leaves my body. I rest back in my seat. Lauren realizes it too and she seems relieved.

"Michael Thomas, huh?" I say.

The baby stretches his hand out to me. He reminds me of a little wolf cub. I offer my hand to the baby. Brian looks like he's gonna kill me if I proceed. The tense pulsing of his temples is a kind of Morse code. "Don't touch him. Do not touch him, you corrupt LA motherfucker," he pulses at me. I hesitate. Both Kelly and Lauren give me the go-ahead with their Morse code temples. I hold Michael Thomas's paw in my hand. "You did real good with this guy, Brian," I say. "You're a lucky guy."

Brian's forehead stops pulsating, his eyes brighten, and the goofiest grin spreads across his face. I honesty did not think Brian's face could contort in such a manner. He looks ugly and beautiful at the same time, like an indigenous statue of a surreal-looking god carved out of wood. "You both did real well," I say to Kelly. The baby blows a little bubble and belches.

Lauren giggles, then Kelly does, then Brian, and then me, too. Our chuckles just get bigger and broader and louder. We can't stop laughing. The baby's face emanates light and that light somehow transfers to all our faces. Everyone is really beaming now. In our dim, little corner of the universe in the French Lounge on French Road in South Cheektowaga, a light beams and even the dark is happy, too, because it's not alone anymore. Lauren reaches across the table still laughing. She touches my hand. I look up and stare right into her eyes but she never looks away like the others before. Kelly sees our exchange and she nods knowingly. There's no hint of sadness or regret in Kelly's eyes. She's happy with her little universe and she should be.

"If you're gonna be in town for a few weeks, we'd love to have you to our home," Kelly says.

Brian nods, approving of Kelly's invitation.

Kelly sweetens the deal. "Lauren'll be there, too."

"Oh, I will, will I?" Lauren retorts.

Kelly teasingly chides her sister, "Don't act like you have anything better to do. If we have a famous writer over to the house, you'll be there." Kelly turns her attention to me. "Lauren's a big reader."

Lauren's beet red.

"I'll come as long as everyone keeps referring to me as a famous writer."

The women don't know how to take my comment, but Brian smirks. This guy gets my humor. I'm liking him more and more. It's been awhile since I've really had a male friend. I know some dude writers but none of them I'd call friends. My writer-friends always seem to be looking for opportunities to kill me when I'm not paying attention. That, I believe, is an evolutionary thing. There're only so many gigs and jobs are survival. What guy wants to go back to their hometown in the Midwest and admit they're a failure?

"I'm joking," I say.

Lauren shifts in her seat and her hip inadvertently touches my hand. I move my hand immediately out of respect. If Lauren notices she's bumped my hand, she doesn't indicate it. Just so you know, Lauren has a firm behind.

"Oh, I get it. You're trying to pretend you're humble," Lauren says.

Lauren's sharp. Very sharp. The funny thing about a lot of the aforementioned asses in Los Angeles is they're actually flabby when you get up close to them. They look good from a distance in their tight bikini bottoms and yoga pants, but up close they're bubbly and gross. It's a rich people thing. Therefore, saggy asses are really an entitlement thing. Lots of LA people think they're so amazing they can have a flabby ass and get away with it.

I'm deeply impressed by Lauren's firm ass and sharp mind. It's obvious. She's a unique person. This awareness leads me to a series of monkey-mind questions. Who is this woman? What does Lauren do for work? Will she sleep with me? Can she solve all my problems? Does she have the ability to help me understand my mother's looming death? What about my own inevitable death? Is she an animal, too?

Buffalo-types, and I mean the good kind like Lauren that aren't decaying like walleye fished out of the icy lake and then forgotten to bake in the sun, realize they have to stay hard in order to survive in this tough world. They don't expect people to kiss their asses if they're flabby. Instead, they're in their frigid homes in their sweatpants and headbands busting their butts to 1980s Jane Fonda's VHS workout tapes their parents bought and forgot about. It finally feels good to be home, among people like Lauren, who, I hope, are a lot like me.

It's almost 1:30 in the morning. Sal never showed. I'm outside the French Lounge in the parking lot. Little Michael Thomas, Kelly, and Brian are long gone. With Kelly and Brian's blessing Lauren's stayed behind, because I promised to be a gentleman and take her home. Despite being a dude and everything, I've vowed to myself to do both – with particular attention to behaving in a gentlemanly manner. I try to respect all women due to my upbringing and the irrepressible urge I have to do the right thing. But when I meet a rarity like Lauren, a really sincere and attractive on all fronts type-human, I feel an even extra sense of responsibility. It's like I turn into a hyper-responsible superhero except I'm only super in neuroticism and I'm addicted to responsibility like it's my last gram of crack.

As far as I can tell, my biggest problem is I am a man. I heard a metaphor once that man is half-animal and half-angel. It's a nice idea, but the percentages are off. I'm assuredly more animal than angel. What angelic creature do you know who farts on command or pretends they are putting out a fire while urinating? To say I have thought with my dick in the past is giving too much credit to the vagina vane/weathercock nearly always protruding from my pants. Lauren touches my shoulder a little heartily.

"Which one's yours?" she asks regarding our mode of transportation.

We've practically shut the place down and there are three cars left in the lot. Thankfully, I'm not drunk. I only had a couple of drinks. The great thing about hanging out with Lauren's family was that neither Brian nor I really had to talk that much. Kelly and Lauren had conversation covered. Sometimes I don't like to talk and prefer to listen. I have a general insecurity about my own words mattering. Maybe that sounds funny coming from someone who is a writer. I don't think so. My insecurity about the frailty of language is precisely why I write. Words are fleeting, meanderings that, even at their best, don't mean much when measured against actions. I don't mind women who talk a lot as long as they're not talking about the latest cult they've joined or the way their asses look in yoga pants or the cost of their Prada bags their mother-in-laws bought for them. So, for me, there are plenty of topics women can cover conversationally and I'm more than happy to listen mostly silently.

"Mine's the Saturn. It's my mother's."

"I used to like Saturns," she says. "No haggling. The problem with most car dealerships is that you're getting screwed no matter where you go. At least Saturn dealers were honest about their prices."

My father would have approved of this woman. "I always thought getting screwed was a way of life," I quip.

"Is that a come on?

"I intended it as more of an existential reality. But if it…"

"I better get home," Lauren states simply as more of an honest truth than a rigid boundary.

A yellow Corvette screams into the lot. Out jumps a young white-dude from the driver-side and Priya from the passenger-side.

The white-dude looks about twenty-five. By white-dude, I mean, he looks Polish. You might be thinking, how can you tell this guy is Polish in the dark and at that distance? It's because I'm an Italian from South Cheektowaga and was completely surrounded by Polish people during my formative years. I can spot a Polish-dude at night from twenty yards distance without straining my eyes. From the moment the Polish-dude hops out of his lame-ass car, he has his nasty little paws all over Priya. He presses her up against the rear of the car and jams his tongue down her throat.

I am becoming rage.

Priya looks over the Polish-dude's shoulder. She sees Lauren and me. Priya looks right in my eyes. She lets the Polish-dude linger for a moment as his hands roam up and down her body and then she pushes him off. I can't tell if her delayed reaction is embarrassment or if she wanted me to watch.

"What are you looking at?" Lauren asks.

"That's my mom's neighbor," I respond.

"The Polish kid?

"No. The Indian girl."

Priya grabs the Polish dude's hand and leads him over to us. "Hi Tommy," she says sweetly as she eyes up Lauren.

"This is Lauren," I grunt in a low voice.

"This is Shane," Priya says nonchalantly.

I fucking hate Shane. I fucking hate every guy I've ever known named Shane! In reality, I've only known two. One was a cross-eyed optometrist who stole my record player; the other a devilishly handsome mechanic who scammed me out of three grand.

"Shane's family owns the pub," Priya says proudly.

"What up, dawg? Shane sneers.

I shake Shane's hand so hard my hand is hurting.

Motherfucker! I can't stand dudes like Shane. His Polish parents own the French Lounge, so, what, he's some damned playboy? You've got to be kidding me. This asshole would fit in perfectly with all the other assholes in Los Angeles. The problem with this asshole in particular, however, is he thinks he's the only asshole in town. Even in Buffalo, he's not. There are plenty of assholes in Buffalo, too, with rich mommies and daddies who give them yellow Corvettes. I can't even afford a Corvette. Not that I'd want one.

"How you doing?" I seethe.

"I'll see you around," Priya says.

"Nice to meet you," Lauren says.

With that, Priya and Fucking-Shane walk off toward the pub. Shane smacks Priya's ass as they enter. I watch as the door slams shut on Priya's innocence.

"She's seventeen," I mumble.

"Kids grow up fast these days," Lauren states.

"I guess. My mom really likes that girl. She'd be disappointed."

"Sometimes you have to kiss a few frogs," Lauren reveals in a knowing way that conveys her own experience. "Shall we?"

I open the car door for Lauren. She enters and I make sure I shut the door softly. I get in and make certain to shut my door delicately, too. The ignition sputters then starts. I back up very slowly like a geriatric and drive cautiously to the parking lot exit. Then, I hit the gas and burn rubber-rage down French Road.

Fuck Shane!

We're driving down French Road toward Union Road. Lauren lives on Caroline Street. A lot of the streets around here have women's first names, like Kathy, Caroline, Tracy, etc. I'm guessing the developers were making a play for 1970s suburban moms looking for a new home in a nice neighborhood. The idea was Caroline Street could be a friend to these fine, fearful white ladies so they wouldn't have to be all by themselves anymore, with only "The Feminine Mystique" and their gin in a coffee cup as their covert companions. Back then, unfortunately, moving to a nice neighborhood really meant a neighborhood with no black people around.

I'm not a fan of these street names. Not only do they reinforce a past that never existed, they also represent an attempt to erase the reality of history from the land. Cheektowaga has a rich history, steeped in Iroquois culture. One thing I've been learning lately is the past always rises up from the burial grounds. I spent my first thirty-seven years like a thoroughbred racehorse running from my past. It's clear to me, now, that I can't escape the ghosts of my ancestors. It's also becoming clearer I'm more of a mutt than a thoroughbred anything.

Lauren listens sympathetically while I verbalize my thoughts about the unfortunate name of her childhood street just as we make it to her house. She takes my ranting in stride and even rants a bit on her own about the injustice of street names and life. Lauren's pretty cool. I think she gets it. Her driveway needs to be plowed and I can't get in, so I park along the curb. Lauren laughs and touches my knee. She's either trying to calm me down or wind me up. It's been my experience with tactile women they are always trying to accomplish one of those things when touching a man. Women must think we're machines they can control. They may be right.

Once, in LA, I was at a restaurant on a first date and my romantic interest slid her hand under the table and, you know, started touching me intimately over my jeans. She went for my zipper but it was totally stuck. Mind you, this was before we ate our main course. It was hot for a moment, until reality kicked in. I didn't want a hand-job, or whatever you call this over-the-pants act, from a stranger in a public place.

My date's grip was overly firm on the part of me she managed to get a hold on. Her movements jerky. I banged my knee on the table in a plea for her to stop, but she read this as a sign I was really into it. What did she do? Firmer and jerkier. Tears were in in my eyes, as I felt beads of sweat roll down my face. She must've read these signs that I was even more into her freaky deal so she redoubled her best efforts.

If only I could orgasm, this situation would be over. But how could I? As the source of my pain, my date didn't provide any inspiration. I tried to imagine someone else. All my exes flashed before my eyes but they did nothing for me. I even remember trying to let my mind wander to celebrities I thought were attractive. But then I started to think about all the medical procedures and exercise routines and general contortions they've had to go through to look the way they look and that didn't work either.

Eventually, I settled on this park alongside the ocean where I used to meditate when I was into self-actualization. Finally, I went totally limp and my date gave up. This woman was really into crystals, too. After dinner, she asked if she could place a crystal on my penis to cure my impotency. At least she asked this time.

I now realize Lauren's trying to calm me down with her tactile approach. She must think I'm getting all worked up about the fascist street names and she doesn't want me to get too upset. I find that most women I come across are notoriously against the revolution. Generalizations are so unfair. I mean, I said most women. You counterpoint with Emma Goldman. I love Emma Goldman as much as anyone. In fact, if I can ever convince a woman to procreate with me and we have a girl-kid, I'll name her Emma after one of the fiercest and most thoughtful anarchists ever. Mental Note, if I ever want to get laid again, and certainly if I want a woman to have a kid with me and stick around to raise it, never mention the word "procreate" aloud in the aforementioned context.

Lauren changes the subject as she asks, "What was the first thing you wrote that you were proud of?"

"I wrote a play. I loved it… the process. I was twenty years old. It was about a bunch of anarchists who take over Buffalo City Hall."

Lauren laughs in a way that's knowing and self-aware. And yes, it can be two things. We have to stop pretending everything is so fucking simple.

"What did you like so much about writing a play?" Lauren asks.

"Hollywood screenplays are pretty formulaic. When writing a play, I could follow my muse."

"Why don't you go back to writing plays then?" Lauren says.

That's a great question. Lauren asks good questions and I'm learning she's a pretty open person, too. Back at the French Lounge she told me she's been living at her parents' home for a few months after leaving a bad marriage. She's a schoolteacher. He was a schoolteacher, too. His name was Brett. That's kind of a douche-name, I think. I put it up there with Shane. It turns out Brett was also a real dick. He had an alcohol problem and slept with one of his students. The girl was only sixteen. Brett was caught with his pants down in the parking lot at the Galleria Mall. I feel bad for the girl. She was just a kid and he should have known better. These things never end well for all involved. Lauren thinks her ex is in Houston, Texas now. Who really knows? I guess Houston's as good as anywhere to run away from yourself. It never works though. At least I don't mess with underage kids.

"That's a good question. When I wrote plays, they weren't very successful."

"Why's that?"

"I'd like to think because they were good, and the world elevates mediocrity more easily. No one makes money writing plays. I ended up moving out to LA, caught a random break, and landed a couple of low paying gigs performing re-writes on scripts. That's been the majority of my writing career for almost ten years. The reality is that hardly anybody makes money writing screenplays either. I've taught classes and done odd jobs to get by. I've been on and off unemployment many times, too. I come back here and feel like a fraud."

Lauren leans in. She's been listening the entire time... really listening. "At least you're living your dream."

"Am I?"

"Well, you're trying. In my book that counts for something."

I laugh Lauren off. She glances out the window and looks back at me. Lauren grabs my hand and holds it. She says, "I've racked my brain over and over about why Brett did what he did. Brett's problem wasn't that he was flawed. It wasn't even that he was self-indulgent. We all have that, I think, to different degrees. It's more that he gave up on his dream. He just stopped trying to be better than what he was."

Lauren looks beautiful to me, and not in some superficial sense. She's beautiful in the sense that I feel less alone right now and maybe she does, and because of that, there is a little more light in the darkness. I kiss Lauren gently on the forehead.

Red lights flash at us from behind. I turn around. It's the police. The Cheektowaga Police Department is a proud organization of the most power-hungry Polish-Americans in the community and other badge-wearing miscreants.

"What's this about?" I say.

The officer walks up to the car. I can see his breath in the air with the streetlight backlighting him. Fittingly, his breath looks a bit blue. He motions for me to roll down the window. I do. He looks right past me at Lauren.

"Everything okay here, ma'am?"

Wait a second, I recognize this face. It's the nose. I've seen this nose before. But the chin's different... Oh my God, it's Pete Karkowski. Pete and I were the same year in school. "Hi Lauren," Pete says. "I didn't know it was you."

Lauren leans across me so she can speak more clearly through the window to Pete. "You remember Tommy. He's back in town to take care of his mom. We met up at the pub and have been catching up. I guess we lost track of time."

"Holy shit, get out of the car!"

I get out of the car, half-wondering if Pete is going to taze me. Pete was a big jock in high school. I wasn't. He had lots of girlfriends. I didn't, but I did okay. Most girls intuitively knew I was going to leave Cheektowaga because of my moderate intelligence and above middling good looks, so a few of them tried to convince me to take them along. Pete played football and lacrosse. I half-remember dating one of his girlfriends and, if I remember correctly, it was after they broke up.

Pete gives me a huge bear hug. Some police tool of Pete's is sticking into my leg as he lifts me right off the ground.

"Is that your flashlight or are you happy to see me," I joke goofily.

"You always were a funny guy." Pete beams.

Out here with Pete in the freezing cold, with our breath blurring into this amorphous blob of blue, I'm again reminded about just how wrong I've been about so many people. Pete is a nice guy. He's a nice, regular guy and there's nothing the matter with that. Being like me, with all the peripatetic thoughts in my mind swirling around like intellectual razors, does not make me superior to anyone else. It also doesn't make me less than anyone either.

Pete's just a man, and I'm only a man, and Lauren's a good woman, too. I have to stop overthinking things.

Judging people for life based on either their first name they had no choice over, or one experience I've shared with them that, in my view, was less than ideal is not fair. Where do I get off convicting people for life on one thing they can't control or an imperfect moment? I'm always making these firm judgments from my own perspective. A viewpoint, mind you, that has become increasingly untrustworthy.

The animal has grown and I don't even know how human I am anymore. If I play the percentage game in my mind, I fear I won't like the balance. When did I start expecting everyone to be perfect? No one in my family is perfect and, believe it or not, I am aware of my own failings despite my bravado to the contrary. I wouldn't appreciate if people judged me on my measure of perfection. In short, I've got to grow up.

"They give you a gun and everything?" I ask Pete.

"Sometimes they even let me fire it."

Damn. Pete's funnier than me, too.

But is it really wrong to strive for perfection? Maybe that's my ego still rearing its fat head, but what would any of us be without our ego? I'll tell you. We'd be our weight in flesh and that's it. In my life, I'm learning that striving to find perfection in others is a colossal failure. But in one's work, what else should we strive for? You can't ask that we totally get rid of our egos but still try to make the world better.

Lauren takes her leave from us boys. "I should get in. I have some papers to grade tomorrow."

"Okay teacher," I say and look over at Pete for the approval I wish I could have received from him in the old days. He smiles back and offers the approval he wishes he gave me or always did, and I was too obtuse to realize.

Pete and I watch as Lauren walks toward her parents' home.

Everything about Lauren is a wave moving in the wrong direction from us; away from me, however temporarily. Lauren looks back at Pete and gives us a wave and a sincere smile.

I look to Pete and it's as if he knows exactly what I'm thinking and it's comforting, like, really, take a nap right out in the freezing cold relaxing. Pete and I are both happy fools out here in the frigid, terrible squalor that is Cheektowaga, and everything is okay for once for a long time for a while.

And I'm not giving up on perfection just yet.

EIGHT
NOT QUITE FOREST LAWN

I'm parked in Camilla's driveway. Despite being drawn in by the solitary hallway light, I can't make myself go inside. I'm wondering if it is okay to really want Lauren even though we only talked for the first time in our lives tonight. Is wanting even a good thing? Desire is suffering, blah, blah, bastardized Buddhism, blah. Connecting with Lauren tonight was a good thing. I'm tired of overthinking good things and not thinking enough before jumping headfirst and knee-deep into bad things. Good is good, right? Spending time with Lauren was good and I felt less alone with her and I'm still feeling less alone right now, and if she had the same experience that's even better. If that's not good, then I don't know what good is anymore. The problem with good things is they feel icky when you're not used to them.

The corvette is in Priya's driveway. Camilla really thinks highly of her. I confess I'm disappointed Mr. Corvette is spending the night. It's not Priya's fault though. Seventeen is a tough age. When I was seventeen, I had no idea who I was and certainly could not figure out other people. Not much has changed in that regard. It's hard all around, and never gets any easier. If I was talking to Priya right now, I might try to explain that to her and hope it provides her some comfort. It sort of did for me when Frank and Camilla each told me the same thing in their own way.

When I was in college, I told Frank I wanted to be a writer. He told me all writers were losers and if I wanted to pursue that track I'd be a loser, too. That wasn't the support I was looking for, but I know now why Frank responded the way he did. He was afraid. Frank wasn't friends with any writers. Hell, he didn't know any writers. Frank didn't want me to become something he didn't know. He thought my wanting to be a writer meant I was moving further away from the neighborhood, from the family, and from him. Dad was right.

I was pre-ordained to be a truck driver or a teacher depending on my ability. But I wanted to be a writer. What the hell was I thinking? Frank was afraid, but so was I. When I approached him, I needed a father's support. I needed his massive biceps and rough hands to hold me up by my armpits if necessary. Instead, his fear won the day. When I confronted him about what he said to me years later (this was a few years before he died), he apologized...well kind of. He said, "I'm sorry, kid, but you can piss on my grave when I'm dead."

After Frank died, Camilla told me she wished she'd divorced my father years earlier. She said there had been someone else she thought she loved. Camilla told me she never betrayed my father. She just wished she'd divorced him and tried things with this other guy. At least that's what she started to say, and then she retracted the whole thing and said she was just grieving, and that "life was hard and that never changes no matter how much living you've done."

I'm in the fields nearby, but not myself. Is this a dream? It's almost dawn. I smell blood and life in my nose, and I like it. Everything is heightened. I feel more alive than usual. My nose is low to the ground as I trot. The smells hit me all at once and it's fantastic. This must be what it feels like to be God. I am so present I feel omnipresent. And bold. I feel bold. Not without fear. There is still fear, but I feel certain of my present task in a way that I have never felt before. My steps are soft and true. The ice cracks beneath me in the underbrush.

A huge wild turkey appears in front of me. Somehow, I knew he was there all along. He speaks to me, "It's good to see you again."

"I've never seen you before," is my instinctual response. My voice sounds craggy and rough. I'm not sure if we're actually speaking words or simply intonations that are understood between us.

"You don't even know who you are anymore." The turkey sounds just like Buffalo R&B legend Rick James.

"You're a wild turkey," I murmur.

"At least you have that down. Baby steps. But I do question the term wild. Who's to say I'm more wild than anything else. I don't know if I should claim the word wild or slap you in the face with my scrotum."

"What am I?" I ask.

"You're on a mission."

"Yes, but what am I?"

"You're some sort of ugly dog or wolf. But that's not important," Turkey sings.

"How did I get here?"

"You know that one. You trotted over here. Get it together!"

"Why am I here?"

"I already told you. You're on a mission, dummy," Turkey laughs.

"What is it?"

"I won't tell."

I show a little fang and move in close. Through my teeth I grimace,

"I'd like to chew on your neck." And I'm not lying. The turkey's neck does look good.

"I was imprecise to say I won't. My words are failing me. I'm sure even a wolf can understand that. It happens to the best of us. What I meant to say is I can't."

"Why not?" I say as I step closer. I can feel my sharp teeth pressing even tighter against my gums.

"These words again. What I'm trying to say is I don't know your exact mission. I just know you're on one. Because you're here. Everyone here is on a mission."

"What's your mission?"

"Leave my mission to me and your mission to you. If they connect, then they're already connecting, baby."

I wake up to Camilla banging on the car window. My head is pounding and the world is in slow motion. Camilla's in her bathrobe but wearing a winter coat and hat. She must have seen me from the window and then put on enough gear to face the elements to see what'd become of me. That tells me she's worried about me, but not too much. If Camilla thought I was dead or something, she would've came flying out of the house wearing only her bathrobe as a Super Mom cape.

"Are you drunk? You're lucky you didn't freeze to death," she says with legitimate annoyance.

She's right. I'm freezing. Did I manage to turn off the car and then pass out? I unlock the door and Camilla opens it up. Cold air rushes in. "I'm sorry, Mom. I fell asleep."

Tough as Camilla is, if she sees her kid's in need, she springs into action. She's always been that way. "Come on," she says and offers her hand.

I take a hold of her mitten and she helps me out of the car.

Every part of me is stiff and sore. Camilla looks at my pants. I'm covered in frozen mud from my ankles near up to my thighs. I was not aware of this before.

"My God, what happened, Tommy?"

"I don't know. Maybe I drank too much," I lie.

"I'm disappointed in you, Thomas."

Uh oh. She called me Thomas. When I was a kid and running late for supper, I'd hear her a block away bellowing from the doorway, "Thomas D'Angelo, get in this house right now or else!" *Or else* had a variety of meanings in my childhood, but generally it meant my mother chasing me around the house with a broom and hitting me. Though I was faster than her, I'd slow down so she could broom me a little – just to get it over with. That's the best thing to do with an Italian mother who's chasing you around the house with a broom. If you don't let her broom you, she'll take it to the next level. The next level for Camilla was the slotted spoon. Part of me is afraid she'll use that spoon on my muddy rump right now.

"I'm really sorry," I say totally afraid and sincere. "I'm supposed to be taking care of you."

Camilla smiles a little but I can tell she's worried. "We can take care of each other." Guilt crashes over me like a wave of plowed snow and nearly topples my weakened, mud-caked vessel. I lean against my dying mother's shoulder as she guides me inside my childhood home. There are tears in my eyes. I try to shield them from my mother but she sees them anyway.

Despite my fierce protestations, Camilla won't leave me alone right now. I'm in the shower. Camilla is sitting on the toilet talking to me. The toilet's not across from me so I have relative privacy. Camilla's afraid I'm going to pass out and die.

"You okay in there?" she asks.

"Yes, Mom."

"I don't think you are. I think you have a problem."

"I'm in the shower and you won't leave me alone. That's my problem," I complain.

"I don't want you to pass out, hit your head, and kill yourself. Your cousin John went like that, you know? I'd like you to outlive me. You need to have kids and carry on the family legacy."

"I'm good. I'm not going to pass out. Do you think maybe I can have some privacy now?"

"Why?" Camilla asks.

"Because this isn't relaxing."

"Your generation relaxes too much. That's why your marriage failed."

"Jesus Christ."

"Don't say His name in vain."

"Can we not talk about my divorce right now?" I beg.

"She was awful. I never liked her, and I'm glad you left her. She relaxed too much."

"I didn't like her either."

"Then why'd you marry her?"

"Existential ache meets desire to hurry inevitable conclusion."

"What the hell does that mean?" Camilla asks.

"It seemed like a good idea at the time."

"When you're feeling better, I want you to take me to your father's grave."

"How come?"

"I need to talk to your father about you."

"You say I have a problem, and you're the one that wants to talk to a gravestone?"

"Not a gravestone. Your father. We have to sort you out. Look at you, you're a mess right now."

The ridiculousness of speaking to my dead father may not be

that bizarre considering the absurdity of all existence. Camilla's right. I can use help by any means I can get it.

"Okay. I'm happy to do that. But privacy, please. I'm begging you."

"Fine. I'll be in the hallway. If I hear a thud or anything, I'll come running."

"When's the last time you went running?"

"You know what I mean. I don't know about all your problems, but one problem I'm sure you have is that you're a smart mouth. Quit being such a smart ass."

I stick my head out of the curtain, glare at Camilla, and do not blink until she leaves the bathroom. Expectedly, she does not close the bathroom door. Exhausted, I sit on the bathtub floor. I let the hot water pour all over my body. When I suffer writer's block, I often break it in the shower. The shower's a magical place where, without even thinking, problems seem to suddenly solve themselves. Unfortunately, I can already tell, the shower's not going to work its magic today.

When I was in the fifth grade, our teachers took our entire class to Forest Lawn Cemetery. If you're someone of importance in Buffalo, it's the place to be buried. Forest Lawn isn't just a cemetery; it's an outdoor museum, too.

I had a friend named Jacob back then. He made an effort to be a good kid. I've always admired the goodness of others even if I can never quite attain the quality myself. But was Jacob really a good kid, or did he just appear to be, given the structure of his upbringing? Jacob was religious. By that I mean Protestant. Most of my schoolmates were Catholic, like me. We went to mass on occasion, and that was the extent of it. But us Catholics knew how to play the religious game. Family turnout for mass was good through the confirmation process. Afterward, our mass attendance declined. Life got in our way. For us Catholics, Buffalo Bills football was our one true religion – on Sundays anyways. So, we identified as Catholic but by most measures we were not religious and did not take religiously principled positions.

For Jacob, that was different. I was shocked when Jacob informed me he was not going on the big field trip to Forest Lawn. He balked at the notion and questioned the entire idea that the trip was academic. The truth is Jacob's parents did not want their son going to the cemetery out of some ridiculous concern our teachers were trying to introduce all of us kids to the occult. It still seems odd to me that religious people, like Jacob's parents, would be so afraid of death. I thought Jesus saved them from all that fear. I can somewhat identify with Jacob's parents. The finality and definitive nature of death is, indeed, frightening.

At Forest Lawn, our teachers had us create gravestone rubbings with construction paper and pencils. We all hurried off to complete our assignment and I ran right into a sculpture of the renowned Seneca Indian Chief Red Jacket. The sculpture impressed me deeply, but at the time I didn't know why. I remember reading the placard next to the sculpture even after my fellow classmates had lost interest. Red Jacket was known as Sagoyewatha or "Keeper Awake." He was famous for speaking well on behalf of his people and, in doing so, could keep everyone's interest. I wonder if that's also true for Camilla. She may not be a great orator but certainly is a persistent one. Perhaps her persistence has kept my father awake all these years.

My father lauded hard work and was fond of saying, "I'll sleep when I'm dead." How disappointed he must be to realize that even in the afterlife there is no rest from Camilla, or from the existential problems of his wannabe writer son. My father's not buried at

Forest Lawn. The D'Angelo family does not have that kind of Buffalo clout. Instead, my father is buried at Briar Lawn Cemetery in Cheektowaga. His father and mother are buried there. Their names were Antonio and Claudia D'Angelo. Claudia's maiden name was Vitala. He's right next to them. Frank was an only son, odd for an Italian family. But I am an only son, too.

Camilla and I stand in front of Frank's gravestone. There's a spot waiting for her beside him. My father was a planner. He bought a plot thinking of her. My father's care for Camilla's grave is both quaint and morbid – a sort of blue-collar romanticism for the post-modern age. Dad's gravestone is small and simple. It's not the intricate type a kid would take a rubbing of on a fifth-grade field trip. There are no decorations on it. Instead, just the basics, name and dates. Keeping it minimal is best. There's no sense in adding additional words on a gravestone. Every part of explaining someone's life on a gravestone is inadequate. Father, son, Buffalo Bills fan, guy who'd beat my behind if I talked back to Camilla, factory worker, recovering alcoholic. None of these words address the totality of Frank nor how quickly he came and went on this earth.

Camilla grabs my hand and holds it beside her. I watch her closely. She mutters incoherently under her breath. For a moment, I can feel Jacob's parents' Protestant paranoia about the occult come over me. Is Camilla really about to channel Frank? That, I cannot handle. The ground rumbles beneath me. Camilla starts to sway back and forth. She's looking at the gravestone lot that will be hers in the near future. A small snowplow truck clears some of the paths nearby. Camilla grabs my arm and holds on.

"Are you all right?" I ask.

"I'm fine. I'm a little tired."

"Do you want me to take you back?"

"Not yet. I'll be okay."

97

My mother turns her attention to my father's gravestone. She looks with love in her eyes. "I'm scared, Frank. Tommy's scared, too. I don't know what to do. You taught me to fight right up until the end, but what happens when there's no more fighting to do?" Camilla leans into me. "Is there anything you want to say to your father?"

"Dad... I can't, Mom. This is too weird."

"Give it a try. He can hear you."

Despite the fact that what Camilla is asking is scientifically impossible and possibly insane, I figure two things. One, Camilla is not going to let me off the hook. Two, fuck it, why not. Life and death are crazy.

I start again, "Dad, I know you weren't always happy with the decisions I made. Maybe you were right about some of those things. I wish I could go back, but I can't. I will take care of Mom. I don't want Mom or you worrying about me."

A serious look comes over Camilla's face and the lines around her mouth tighten as she says, "Your father was always proud of you. Tell him, Frank."

We wait there in silence for what feels like an entire Buffalo winter. A gust of wind whips up and knocks the fedora hat cockeyed on my head. The hat's location makes a sort of seashell tunnel in my ear and I swear I almost hear the wind say in a breathy voice, "Always proud."

This fedora was my father's hat. I hadn't even remembered I was wearing it. Camilla placed it on my head as we walked out of the house. I always hated that fedora growing up. It embarrassed me because I thought my father looked silly in it. I dare not fix the hat on my head myself. Camilla adjusts the fedora but leaves it slightly askew like my father used to wear it. I look more like a wannabe gangster than a wannabe writer. What does it matter? Camilla is right. No matter what, my father has always been proud of me. Deep down, I've always been proud of Frank and Camilla, too. My father and mother were proud people and loyal. They were tough on me but they were fair. They worked hard and they loved each other and their only son. It's hard to put all that on a gravestone. I wouldn't dare try.

It's also really hard to speak about both of my parents in the past tense. I hope Camilla can stay with me for a little while longer.

NINE

A GRAND TEST

Fuck. I'm in the fields again, trotting. I guess this is my thing now — running around in the fields as some sort of badass animal. The moon is growing full and I have one eye on it no matter where I am. Where the hell is that wild turkey? I have so many questions for that guy. Something tells me he has all the answers I'll ever need. It's either that or this other competing desire is driving me, rising to the surface like a dead body in a swamp. I think I really want to eat that turkey. The first opportunity I get, I want to sink my teeth into its gooiest vital bits. Then, I want to rip it apart piece by piece, violently, viciously, and without any glimmer of inhibition. When the turkey's dead and after I've eaten him to the point I might hurl if I have one more bite, I want to lay right next to his remaining carcass and lick my paws and every once in a while, nibble the remaining gristle just to remind myself I killed him, and to put on notice any other scavenger motherfuckers lurking around that I'm not finished with my fucking meal.

Something hits me in my hindquarters and I turn in time to see the wild turkey's beak receding from just having pecked my ass. I twirl and snap, like a pup after his own tail. Before I can bite the turkey's nape, he's up in a tree and on a branch just sitting there staring at me. I didn't know turkeys could fly. Maybe this is a special turkey. The turkey's arrogantly laughing as I jump up again trying to reach him. "Are you a turkey God?" I ask.

"Of course I am. We all are."

What a prick. How dare this turkey taunt me? If this ecosystem is a body, then this turkey is its asshole. I snap at him again, but overreach and fall on my backside. "Hey, I've been wanting to eat you. I mean talk to you."

"I can see that," Turkey states.

"I didn't know turkeys could fly."

"Of course we can, baby. I'm flying all day long."

"I need to know my mission, man," I bark.

"You're going to be tested."

"I'm being tested right now."

"No. This is nothing. You think you want up here. But you don't. If you made it all the way up here with me, you'd just have farther to fall."

"I have an idea then. You come down here. We talk awhile like old friends. Then I eat you," I suggest.

"Everything is always happening, man. But that ain't happening."

"Fine. Anybody ever tell you that you sound just like Rick James?"

"You're the super freak around here, baby wolf man."

It's about dinnertime and I'm driving around in Camilla's Saturn on French Road. I have a thing with Lauren. I'm not sure if it's really a date or not. She called and asked me to go out to dinner. "Super Freak" is blaring from the speakers. The windows are down because I'm feeling warm despite the fact it's a high of thirty-three degrees today. I should probably mention I'm smacking my hand on the wheel with the beat and singing along.

By the second verse, I'm somehow shaking my ass in my seat and my shoulders are bouncing along with the rhythm. There's a red light so I stop. I just keep on singing and shaking. Suddenly I hear another voice singing along with me as the chorus kicks in. Is it God? Is it the wild turkey? The sound is not coming from inside my mind. I turn my head to the right and see a cop car. Pete's singing along.

"Where you off to?" Pete asks.

"Heading to Lauren's."

"Go get her, Tiger."

Corresponding with tiger, Pete hisses like a cat and motions with his claw. The light turns green. Pete speeds ahead, waves for me to follow and flashes his lights. I follow him all the way to Lauren's parents' house. Pete waves goodbye with his cat-claw and hisses off.

I don't know how to take Pete's behavior. Maybe this is how all Cheektowaga cops act and I've been away too long to remember.

As I walk up Lauren's driveway – now immaculately plowed – I sense a kindred spirit in the premises. I step to the door and hear a dog bark from inside. Lauren greets me before I can even ring the bell. A huge, older German shepherd greets me. Lauren holds him back as he obligatorily barks. Lauren opens the door as she says, "This is Otis. He's mine, not my parents'. He's friendly." Otis doesn't seem overly friendly as he lunges and snaps at me. She pulls him back. "As soon as you get in the house, he'll be fine." I wonder if Otis recognizes a fellow Canidae family member and sees me as a challenge to his place in the pack. I enter. Lauren's right. Otis calms right down. He immediately licks my hand. I get down on his level and pet him. He lumbers to his side and gives me his tummy to pet. I don't disappoint him.

From my position down on the floor I look up at Lauren and really see her for the first time. Let's call it our first contact. I can tell she's rattled. The dog doesn't have her that way because he's already calm. I say first contact because despite our previous closeness, I now feel as though one of us is an alien. It may be due to her hairstyle. Lauren's hair is bigger than I remember. Much bigger. She must have used some sort of hairspray to puff it up. Her hair reminds me of the '90s in Cheektowaga which was much like the '80s everywhere else. You have to remember, a place like Cheektowaga is at least a decade behind either of the coasts.

Lauren speaks out, "My parents would like us to stay for dinner instead. I'm really sorry. Is that okay? I couldn't talk them down." That's what has her rattled. Her parents.

"Sure," I say. But it is not okay. It's actually the last thing I want to do and I didn't even know it was the very last thing until Lauren uttered it.

As soon as I walk past Lauren's alien hair and deeper into the foyer, I realize her parents' home has the exact same layout as my parents'. The same contractor built both of our homes. That said, Lauren's parents' home is quite different from my childhood home, at least superficially. There are no knickknacks on the walls. Everything is super clean.

Lauren takes my coat and places it in the closet as if we were twenty years married and this is common practice. From this angle, I see her behind for the first time this evening. It does not look as proud to me as the night before. My heart beats fast. Was the other night a lie? Did I yet again turn Lauren into the woman I wanted her to be rather than the person that she is truly? Am I a superficial piece of shit for freaking out because her ass is not as momentarily attractive to me right now? I don't know if I can do it. I don't know if I can live with an ass I'm not always attracted to for the rest of my fucking life!

Lauren touches my arm like she knows what I'm thinking and

pities my neurotic fears. She looks in my eyes like I'd imagine a true saint would to an untrue sinner.

I calm down a notch. She smiles warmly and gestures for me to follow her up a couple of stairs and into the living room. Otis follows us, too. I check out Lauren's butt again. Otis sees me looking and gives me a knowing glance. I realize Lauren's pants aren't as flattering as the night before but she still has a great ass. Thank God. I pat Otis on the head and wink at the crucifix in the living room on our way toward the adjacent dining room.

Lauren's parents are already sitting. Her mother is giving a neck rub to her father who is seated at the head of the table. "These are my parents," she announces grandly. "Mom and Dad, this is Tommy."

Lauren's father grimaces at me. I think he hates me. That's fair. He knows I have a penis and firsthand how obtuse those little peckers can be. Lauren's mother tightly smiles through all the following, "I'm Denise and this is Bob. So pleased to meet you. Bob threw out his back shoveling. The snow blower broke a month ago but he still won't fix it."

"We don't have the money," Bob grunts.

"We have it," Denise responds through a taut smile.

Lauren looks horrified. I know that look of utter mortification, having experienced it among my family many times before.

I stick out my hand to Bob to break the tension. Denise takes it instead and shakes it too enthusiastically as she says, "Bob can't lift his arm because of his back. Maybe we'll get the snow blower now. We're so honored to have a writer in our home. So very honored."

Bob looks at Denise and says, "I wouldn't have bothered shoveling the snow." He glares at me. "If it wasn't for the company coming over last minute. It's all supposed to melt tomorrow."

Denise clutches my arm desperately as if clinging to her last shred of keeping it all together as she whispers in my ear, "Have a seat, dear."

I take my seat. Lauren sits next to me. Otis takes his spot between us under the table.

Forks and knives scratch on the Townsend's plates as I stoically stare at the venison on my own. Denise slices through the tension. "Bob shot this deer himself."

"Tommy is a vegetarian," Lauren reports.

"Oh, how interesting," Denise responds.

Bob grunts at me with ice in his eyes. I guess eating the venison is some sort of man-test. He can die holding his breath before I eat any for all I care. It's well established I am the most stubborn animal in the universe. Just ask the wild turkey in the woods. I grab a cloth napkin off the table and sneak a little piece of venison in it. My co-conspirator gobbles it up under the table. Otis keeps cool, so no one notices. I like this dog. He'd be good in a pinch.

Denise screws her smile even tighter to try to contain all the tension beneath the surface of the dinner table. Lauren tries not to break down in tears. Bob tips back another beer. I stare at the venison. The animal part of me is craving it. Craving it bad. I want its flesh and blood. It should have been my kill and not Bob's. Who the fuck is he anyway? Bob's not a sliver of the hunter that I am. The guy has a bad back. He's fat and old. Bob's no longer pack leader. His problem is he just doesn't know it yet. That will be his downfall. It's the demise of all the once powerful, now burdened with the decay of their marrow. Evolutionarily, Bob's already dead. If we were in the frigid wild where I belong, I wouldn't bother to kill Bob to take over the pack. I wouldn't need to. We'd just be walking, walking, walking, and finally he wouldn't be able to keep up and he'd command me to stop, but the pack would look to me for direction and we'd walk on. I wouldn't even look back in the pack's wake to see that Bob's a frozen meat Popsicle. This is my venison at the table to offer to whom I please.

Nothing's particularly interesting about the conversation. It's not pleasant or stimulating. Grunts from Bob, forced grins from Denise, and grimaces from Lauren are the primary methods of communication. I don't say much mostly because I don't have anything much to say. This family archetype led me to move twenty-five hundred miles away in the first place. Just like Frank and Camilla, Bob and Denise will never really get me. I'm the alien animal to them all, including Lauren. She can try to be an alien like me, with her alien hair, but she can't ever be like me. Why? Because I'm a dick wagging fucking wild wolf man, that's why. I can't be tamed.

The conversation is white noise anyway, because this dinner table is a time machine and I keep intermittently transporting back in time to my childhood home. I'm eight years old. Frank is drinking too much and Camilla is giving him shit about it with her unsubtle looks, and Jesus, from high upon the wall, is giving us all shit about our general depravity with his own disapproving looks.

This is before Frank exiled the crucifix. But I now understand its banishment. It wasn't only that Camilla was bound to the crucifix in the suffering of her miscarriages; Frank looked at the crucifix and saw God's judgment. Dad wasn't just a hardheaded drinker. He drank through his suffering. Frank drank through what he, on some dark inner-level, believed to be his failure as a man. Dad felt he failed to protect his unborn children from the arbitrary cruelty of the world. It didn't matter that Frank was expecting too much of himself. Life is fragile, after all. Frank was an unreasonable man with unreasonable expectations. But aren't we all? A miscarriage is no one's fault. Either that or it's the fault of God. But God does not accept responsibility for God's actions because God is God. I'd wash my hands of everything if I were God, too.

Frank transferred his own sense of judgment into the crucifix.

He saw Jesus judging him because he held himself accountable for what was beyond his control. The ironic thing in life is it is man's unreasonable nature that brings the most kinesthetic energy. Yes, it can lead to self-destruction. But it also can lead to greatness. It is the unreasonable person who completes not only the necessary tasks for survival but also those tasks that transcend survival and enter the realm of the spiritual.

Bob grumbles across the table in a pained voice resembling a bear furious with an impossible itch on his blubbery back, "You haven't eaten any venison, Thomas."

Why is Bob calling me Thomas? Bob has no idea who the fuck he's dealing with. Maybe he shot that venison from thirty yards away, maybe forty. But I kill up close.

I take a slab of venison off the plate with my bare hand. I rip it in half. I jam the larger portion into my mouth. The bloody juices run down my chin. I smile at Bob and then Denise and Lauren and show my fangs as I speak through chomps. "It's delicious."

Dinner's over. I make a hasty retreat. Lauren and I are alone at the door, except for Otis who stands in the living room looking regally down the stairs at us. He must feel like he's the king and we are his fools with such silly concerns about what we believe really matters. Lauren gives me my coat in silence and I put it on. Otis pants. I pull my dad's fedora down low as a signal I don't really want to talk.

"You didn't have to eat the venison," she says.

"I know."

"My dad... This is just his way of being protective. He doesn't want to see me hurt again."

Before even thinking I retort, "Your ex hurt you, and I get that, and I'm sorry for that. But your ex hurting you doesn't have a damned thing to do with me." Wow. That was honest. Years ago, I would have laid down and taken someone else's beating because I thought that would help the person I loved, and I'd come back for more like a dog more loyal than concerned for his own good. But I've changed.

Am I being too hard on Lauren considering the sloshing mess going on in my brain? There are raw places within I wouldn't want anyone to know about; much less criticize. Who am I to judge? There are two points to mull over. Number One, everyone has dark and messy stuff inside. To pretend it's not there doesn't make it go away. Each person is filled with animal and muddy angel thoughts competing for supremacy in each slipping conscious to unconscious moment. Number Two, everyone has the right to judge other's behavior as it pertains to them. That's about survival.

That sort of judgment can't be taken away from people. To do so is to strip them naked in the wild in the tall grass in a long drought and light a match. The religious try to do it. The liberals try to do it. The conservatives, too. All the fakers try. They pretend judgment is an evil thing. Meanwhile, they judge all the time based upon behaviors that have nothing to do with them.

If people want to serve a magical God, so be it. If they want to shoot a gun, so be it. If they want to be gay, so be it. Worship a gun while having gay sex for all I care as long as it doesn't affect me. But expect a very different response if the intention is to stick the god gun up my ass and pull the trigger. Then, I have every right to judge and every right to respond with a shrill, shrieking, "Back the fuck off motherfucker!" In fact, I have an evolutionary responsibility to do so.

I wear my sort of judgment proudly like Sunday clothes for the church I never attend. Better yet, I carry this judgment around like a club. When I sleep, it's right next to me, so if someone comes at me funny in the night, I'm ready to parlay their misdirected projected onslaught and crack them right between their fucking eyes.

Other people's past business is not my concern. My past might taunt me or haunt me. My past might ride on my back like I'm the world's wackiest jackass or stick out my side like a bastard appendage I wish I had the courage to cut off with a broadsword. My past might pry open my head with its skeleton vulture hands, stick in its creepy claws, and squish my brain into a thought puddle. But it's my past. I deal with my own shit and try my damnedest not to put it on others. The only rule is people who want to ride in close proximity to my flesh carriage carry around their own shit and dump it off to the side if they need. Just don't toss it on my hipster boots when I'm trying to walk down my path which is my path alone and I have no idea where I'm going, but I keep on walking one step at a time. Given the solitary and unclear path we must travel, it's hard enough without dodging other people's shit or being asked to carry it in our heads.

I give Lauren a kiss on the forehead. There is gentleness and distance like a father might feel for his daughter. I don't feel paternal toward Lauren, nor do I feel more enlightened than her. But I do feel the distance between us that's been caused by Lauren projecting onto the present something from the past. I've responded with a boundary and that might feel paternalistic even though it's simply self-care. And I do still care for Lauren, too. In my past experiences, I've found that projection causes distance of an unhealthy variety, and it cannot be accepted. I categorically unequivocally fucking refuse. Judge me fully on my actions and how they impact the relationship. But I refuse to be judged based upon someone else's failings who came before me.

Lauren looks up at me and I can see the concern in her eyes that I might never come back to her house for dinner or anything ever again. Her fear is rational.

"Thank you for coming to dinner," she says.

I look directly at her. "Thank you for having me."

Lauren can see in my eyes that years earlier I took someone

else's beatings because I thought that was love. That was not my responsibility. But I've come back to Buffalo to accept responsibility for what is right for me to carry as a son. With trepidation and fear, yes. But I'm stronger now. I know what responsibility is mine and I also know the crosses that are not mine to carry.

Even though Christ was on and off my parents' walls throughout my upbringing, the metaphor of Christ remained. He was ever the martyr for my family, giving of his flesh and blood to save all the sad sacks who projected their sins upon his torn up visage. Internalizing being like Christ meant accepting the projection of other people's poor behaviors. I thought I could carry their pain so that the people I loved could be free from suffering. It was a damn stupid fucking idea, and self-destructive as hell.

I don't know if I'll see Lauren again. But I'm not running away either. I don't expect people to be perfect and I am hopeful that people can change. Otis bounds down the stairs. I say goodbye to him by tickling the fur on the side of his neck and patting his head. He's a good dog and I hope I'll see him again. I give Lauren a hug and neither of us lingers. She doesn't hold on to me too long, and I appreciate it. We both have thinking to do.

At a casual pace, I walk out the door. Part of me feels like the door closing behind me is also closing a chapter of a family legacy bigger than my life experiences alone. This has much less to do with Lauren and much more to do with my own self-awareness. I'm not the same man I was. Despite my every human impulse to avoid change, I have, indeed, changed. When something is unhealthy, I can recognize it now. I'm able to name it directly without freaking the fuck out. Walking away is acceptable. But I'm not running, and the door is always open for change.

The streetlight flickers and goes off as I pull into Camilla's driveway.

It's only around 9:00 p.m. but it's as black out as a werewolf's heart. The fields call me. It's as if its voice is inside my blood. I look over to Priya's house and wonder what she's up to tonight. She's probably out with that fucking Polish kid, Shane, whose family owns the French Lounge. Shane's no good for her. But it's not my problem.

Priya's garage door opens mechanically with a little hitch in the middle. Sal's truck backs out. I can't see Sal's face clearly in the darkness but I can tell it's his squirrelly little ass in there. Is Priya hooking up with Sal? That motherfucker, Sal. He has no respect for anything sacred; for anything innocent in this savage cesspool world. It's like the entire fucking world's become the black curbside sludge caked on old snow. Sal drives up Crabapple Court away from Camilla's. I don't think he saw me. If he did, he sure didn't want to stop to say hello.

My cell phone rings. I don't recognize the number. Maybe Sal has a cell after all and he saw me and he's calling to try to explain the whole thing; that whatever I'm thinking about him and Priya is a terrible misunderstanding, and he's just been looking in on the Indian kids for their welfare, and I don't need to say anything to Camilla. I answer the call, but can't make out any words right away. It's a girl's voice. The nasal quality tips off it's Priya.

"I see you in your car," she says.

I watch the curtains casually draw open and Priya's silhouette teases me.

"How did you get my number?" I ask.

"Sal gave it to me. I need to talk to you... in person."

"I don't think that's a good idea."

"Why not?"

I sure as hell know why not. It's not my place to go over to a seventeen-year-old girl's house at 9:00 p.m., or ever. I don't want to say that to her, however. So, I say something lame. "My mom needs me."

"Well, I need to talk to you face to face. It's important."

This conversation reminds me of many I had with my ex-wife, who can best be described as a marginally intelligent, partially conscious, manipulative butter knife in a flattering dress. It's the manipulation covered in something sweet. Despite my concern, my interest has already been piqued. I need to find out what Sal is up to. Neel and Priya must be protected from Sal's nefarious ways. My father, Frank, looked in on Audrey and Sal out of his own sense of duty when Big Sal ran out on them. That's what this is about for me. It's my duty to care for Neel and Priya, whose parents left them among the Cheektowaga deviants so they can live the high life in India. Cut to an old Indian couple popping Champagne while swinging from a crystal chandelier in a Bollywood musical. Back to reality. That's why I'm piquing dammit. I'm here for these Indian kids. Back the fuck off, conscience.

"Fine," I say to Priya.

I hang up the phone and take a deep breath.

As I walk up to Priya's door, I hear three distinct sounds blending together in a discomforting cacophony. The first is some sort of loud techno music. The second is a continuous, orgasmic, nasally female voice. The third is the intermittent sound of, what I think are, bursts of machine gun fire and subsequent shell cases clanging on the floor over and over. I don't duck for cover because I've heard this sound before. Back in Los Angeles, my ex-convict neighbor is a gamer. He plays the same video game. The breathy voice belongs to some video game prostitute who needs saving. Though it is super annoying to listen to the sound of machine gun fire all day when you're trying to write, I never say anything. I don't think that makes me a coward. It makes me smart. During the day he's an ex-con with a big smile, but at night he gets drunk and rages.

The door's cracked open and a reddish light from inside the

house spills out. I knock on the door. Not hearing any movement, I knock again. There's still nothing but the techno and the video game. I knock once more. Again nothing. I call Priya on her cell. She doesn't pick up. Now I'm getting a little worried. What if something terrible has happened? Maybe she slipped and fell and she can't hear me because of all the noise.

I slowly open the door. The house has the same layout as Camilla's except it's in reverse. It's fairly dark but that red-hued light is coming from the living room. The walls are a light shade of red. The rug is a deeper shade of the same. There are colorful hangings on the walls that are purplish mixed with turquoise and yellow. My eye is drawn to an altar with a statue on it. It's, Rati, the Hindu goddess of love and sexual arousal. She stands proudly, bow in hand with two arrows strung and ready to shoot from her perch on top of a bunch of naked women, their bodies all interconnected. One bare breasted woman raises her right hand to the heavens; another's on all fours with a woman riding her; and another woman's legs are spread wide open invitingly with a fourth woman laying comfortably between them.

From behind me I hear movement. I turn in time to see Priya entering the living room from the bathroom. She's wearing a periwinkle nightgown, more like a bathrobe, that's a little too big. My first thought is that it must be her mother's.

"Don't worry," she seduces. "He's in his room."

The words that she's saying are not making any sense in my sprinting-a-marathon-in-a-moment monkey-brain. "What?" I mutter.

"Neel's in his room."

Priya's hand moves toward the bathrobe belt. I put up my right hand like a traffic cop to get her to stop. Before I can say anything, she's undone the belt and slips right out of the robe. She's blindingly, stark naked. I see everything in red shadow. This is the moment of truth.

Though the moment seems to go on forever in my brain, it does not. Not only do I immediately avert my gaze, I close my eyes, too. While doing so, I'm involuntarily stammering, "No, no, no." I can't see a fucking thing as I smack into the wall and bump the statue of Rati. It doesn't fall to the floor. I feel my way to the door.

"What's wrong?" Priya asks.

Even in this perfect paradoxical place of absolute chaos and resolute clarity, I feel for her. Priya's only a kid and she's just been incredibly vulnerable, but she's also mistaken. This entire thing has been one colossal, cluster-fuck, Bay of Pigs, Bay of fucking Pigs, Iraq War, George W. Bush mistake. My hand is over my eyes now.

I tell her, "Nothing's wrong. You're a very lovely person, and that's why I can't. That's why we can't. It's about respect for you and I need you to know that!" I hope I'm not shouting at her. But I'm incredibly stressed out and that may have been me shouting. Am I screaming? I stumble out the door. "We can talk about this later."

Like a drunken fool, I stagger through the series of front yards toward the safety of Camilla's. I run into a gnome in one yard, and a plastic Santa Claus, and an entire Nativity scene in the next. In my stupor, I knock both Santa and baby Jesus to the ground. I try to pick them back up in an effort to leave no saint nor God behind but I fail with Santa and drop him back to the ground. Sorry, Santa, I've got to get the fuck out of here. At least I've saved you, Baby Jesus. Out of the corner of my eye I see the wild turkey, Oliver. The son of a bitch is laughing at me. In an instant, he disappears. I haul ass inside the safety of Camilla's home.

TEN

CAMILLA'S SONG

I wake up in the morning to the sound of "Over the Rainbow." Mom's alto voice carries throughout the entire house. It's one of the songs that really suits her vocal register, like it was made for her to sing by a god that cares about such details. Songs are funny that way. If sung repetitively to the point where these songs reach a creation threshold, they become the projected soundtrack of one's life. That's how human beings change the world. We project an inward vision outward until the physical world bends and folds and builds to make that expression exist in the real. This is the power we have that's different from other animals. It's a wonderful and terrible power.

Despite everything, Camilla and I are alive in Cheektowaga this morning. If there is a deity planting tiny songs in our brains like a distant gardener or whether we create our own songs without any help, life still matters as long as we decide it does. And if there really is nothing but wonderful, terrifying emptiness in the thereafter, I think life is worth quite a bit. I don't know much about heaven, but, like in "The Wizard of Oz," I'm guessing the wizard is not the dude we think. People act like the wizard is this moral wall to push off that lets us know the boundaries around what is right and what is wrong. But I didn't run away from Priya out of fear for burning in hell in the thereafter.

Hell doesn't scare me because I've already been to two places people claim are worse than "hell." The first one is in the San Fernando Valley, known as "The Valley." People say it's "hotter than hell" there. They're not lying. It is hellaciously hot in The Valley, but there are plenty of strip malls where you can easily get to all your favorite air-conditioned chain stores for respite. The second place supposedly worse than hell is right here in Cheektowaga, New York. People always say it's "colder than hell" here. They're not lying either. Cheektowaga offers the kind of colder-than-a-witch's-tit-winter-hell that shrinks men's testicles and hardens women's nipples (not erotically). But Cheektowaga, like The Valley, also offers a variety of strip malls. And in these strip malls you can warm up and consume all the things you've never needed. In truth, The Valley and Cheektowaga are terrible places to live but the people who survive there are pretty nice. So, I'm not afraid of hell, and fear of hell did not influence my running away from Priya.

I ran away from Priya because we are both human beings and I empathized with her position as a fellow angel/animal struggling for self-actualization within a society set-up to keep us from our truth. Society says if she is eighteen it's cool for us to have sex, but if she is seventeen it's not. The rules can be confusing that way. But power dynamics with relationships, sexual or otherwise, are real, and imbalances can have devastating consequences. Children ought to be protected from people who might abuse their position of power over them. It's as simple as that, despite our supposed animal impulses.

The common popular culture myth is our animal brain nearly always says yes to sexual opportunities, especially for men. That lie suggests a man will automatically have sex with any woman he finds attractive. For a man, that's supposed to be most women given that mythology. In the situation at Priya's house, evolution said to my animal brain she might be a good vessel for my offspring. But that wasn't the only factor under consideration. Though on some level my animal brain wanted sex with Priya for purposes of procreation, my animal brain also led me to run the hell away when presented with that chance. There was no conscious, rational thinking about why not to have sex with Priya as I closed my eyes and stumbled out of the room – like a stoned saint on a pilgrimage to the great truth out in the dark among the plastic lawn ornaments. Pure instinct charted my course. My empathy for Priya informed instantly and unconsciously that looking at her naked body and more so enjoying it, and all the fleeting pleasure that entails, was not right for her or for me.

I didn't run because she is the virginal saint in my mind and I am the sinner. It wasn't because she disappointed me with her naive, intense sexuality, or that I suddenly found myself with an unfair sexual repulsion upon discovering Priya may not be as virginal as I had previously fantasized. No. I ran because my animal brain instinctually realized Priya's a lost animal/angel in the dark, seeking the truth for whatever that's worth. And if she's special, she's unique in the way we all are. We are all so lost its beautifully maddening and all we can do is try to find our way in or through or by. If we're all lost out here in the muck and grabbing for passing, shrinking little shadows to hold onto in the pain and despair, at least my animal brain guided me to not do anything that might make Priya's journey more difficult.

A crash of a breaking plate sounds from below. Is Camilla okay?

"Son of a bitch!" she yells.

Mom's fine. She restarts her song. Life is hard enough. That's right. It's hard enough without adding to the confusion. There's the whole mortality thing for us animal/angels to consider. Then there is the existence question. Then there's the question of if anything really matters. And then there's the question of whether there is any meaningful order to life or if it's all chaos. Finally, there's the question of connection. Are we bound to each other or not? The animal in me resoundingly says yes. It growls we are all connected, so treat each other well in the darkness.

What if I'm wrong about my animal brain and ran for pure evolutionary survival? So what. I like to think we're all connected. Even if we're not, I do know I find existence difficult and I prefer not to add to the hardship for others. Wouldn't Cheektowaga be a better place if we all took the approach we are connected to each other and ought, in the least, to do no harm and, at most, to help others who are actually slivers of ourselves on their way down the unsure path?

We appear on the path coming from nothing; all of us bastards alike. Who made us? We don't know. We don't know where the path goes. But we're on it, nonetheless. At least we feel like we are on a path leading to a conclusion. We call it death but the word is an abstraction. Thinking of the end creates fear. So, our feet keep marching steadily forward to a distant rhythm that somehow comes from within us. Is there life after? Who cares? People making money off our fear care the most. The majority of us want to stay around as long as we can and have a few laughs along the way.

I hear my mother crooning downstairs, building momentum through the very end of her song.

Camilla's asked me to take her to see her cardiac specialist at Buffalo General Medical Center. It's the first time she's let me in about her illness since I've been back home. The truth is I'm happy to help. I recognize I've been roaming about town like a conspiratorial vagabond. Like a teenage pup feeling his masculinity for the first time, I've been testing it out on the wrong occasions. All of the above is complicated. But part of my return home to misadventures of the mundane and absurd is because I've wanted to be a support to Camilla but haven't known how. On one hand, she's been keeping me at bay. On the other hand, I haven't known how to communicate I want to help. I'm grateful she's asked me to take her to the appointment. Being Camilla's chauffeur to Buffalo General is something that feels marginally useful.

Buff General's not in the best neighborhood in the city. You can tell this neighborhood used to be something pretty nice years ago. Huge old homes, now dilapidated, line the streets en route to the hospital. A bunch of mentally ill transients walk around nearby. Many of them must innately feel they need help and congregate around the radius of the hospital, drawn to it like moths to a flame. Camilla and I are not too unlike these hobos. We're all wandering around the hospitals in our own lives; aware we need help, yet avoiding asking for it as long as possible. These mentally ill transients might be shamans in a different society less focused on uniformity of thought.

As Camilla and I step out of the car in the parking lot, there's a police helicopter circling around the neighborhood. Camilla covers her ears as I look up. The chopper puts me on edge. The cops must be looking for someone. A transient gentleman wearing shorts over his jeans walks past me shaking his fist at the copter as he complains, "Goddamn helicopter. Makes everyone get all up in a cramp. They should take that guy's fucking license away." I find insane people like this chap have the sanest ideas. If it were up to me, I'd make this gentleman the mayor.

I walk Camilla, arm in arm, up the causeway to the hospital. The way the hospital is built creates a wind tunnel at the entrance. It feels like all the wind blowing off Lake Erie is funneled down this small walkway right at us. The current is always at your face as you enter and at your back on the way out. This wind tunnel is an unfortunate externalization of the realities at many hospitals. It's hard to get help when you need it. First, you have to overcome denial of your suffering. Next, you have to overcome your own desire for self-reliance. Then, you have to overcome institutional ineptitude at best and outright malice for the underclass at worst. When you overcome all that mess and get the minimal help you need, the hospital/insurance corporate nexus is kicking your ass to the curb as fast as irresponsibly allowable, and the wind's there for a little extra shove to help you on your way out.

We make it inside the lobby. A nun walks toward us, greets us, and tells us she'll pray for us. The nun gives me a little pamphlet with Jesus on the cover. You can see right into his chest to his heart. His heart's not anatomically correct. I suppose this fake heart is supposed to be a symbol for Jesus that goes beyond the corporeal. Frank would have approved of this bloodless heart because at least it is not gruesome. But it's also not a real heart. Honestly, I think this fake heart does Jesus a real disservice. Jesus had a body and he suffered. That's the thing we have in common with him the most. My mother needs help with her actual heart in this place. Curing a symbol of her body isn't going to do shit for her. That's the rope-a-dope trick religion plays to fool you into temporarily feeling better which is actually the trick they play to convince you of their God-given ability to do so.

If you come in needing help for your body, the religious point to your mind. If you need help with your mind, they point to your body. If you ask a question about reality, they offer an answer about spirituality. Camilla smiles a little nervously, afraid I might say something inappropriate to the nun. I stand there like a holy goof because I can't formulate an intelligible response and simply saying thank you for this pamphlet is inadequate. With a knowing nod, the nun quickly moves on. This is not out of disrespect or insincerity from the nun. There is simply so much suffering here that she is very busy.

Camilla and I make our way through the lobby where there is a small stand selling hospital essentials: coffee, candy bars, flowers, cards, etc. Out of the corner of my eye, I notice a newspaper and think about Sal. What is he up to? Camilla and I enter the elevator. I press number ten to take us up to the cardiac floor. At least the elevator is going up without a hitch. Maybe that's a good omen.

Dinesh Rath is the name of Camilla's doctor. I shake his hand and my first ignorant thought is wondering if he is a friend of Priya's since he's Indian. Then, I have this irrational fear he knows I saw Priya naked because they must have talked about it – since they're both Indian. I worry even though I didn't enjoy it and ran the hell out of there, he's still pissed off and is going to take it out on Camilla by withholding his healing powers. But Dinesh small-talks about the Buffalo Bills and tells me that he studied in London but is originally from Pakistan. So, I decide I'm going to let the Priya thing go for now. They probably don't know each other after all since he's from Pakistan. In other words, I let my second ignorant anxiety-ridden thought let me off the hook for my first. When Camilla tells Dinesh I'm a writer, he seems very impressed.

"Books?" he asks.

"Movies."

"Ah… writing images. That's where it's at, man. The world is all pictures now."

"You'd think that would make it easier," I mutter as I look toward my mother. For a moment, I almost think I see her heart rising from her chest.

"It doesn't?"

I want to connect but it comes out as a rant. "You take an exploitative business and then add in the glut of images via the proliferation of the digital age and the exploiters can further justify the degradation of labor of those who have the skill-set to write images into existence."

"I get it, man. As a doctor, I don't have that tyranny, but I get it. We get to work on the body. For people our work is very present, and people will pay for that." Dinesh looks at Camilla and then lowers his eyes a bit slightly to the side. "But we have other tyrannies, man."

I went into this meeting expecting not to like Dinesh. To the contrary, I like him very much. He's a smart guy who gets it, man. I bet we could be friends. He's friendly and he's sincere, much like the nun from the lobby. Like the nun, unfortunately, the problem with Dinesh is he can't solve Camilla's health problem despite his best offering. The nun offers something spiritual when Camilla needs something physical. Dinesh works in the physical realm, but that realm has its limitations. He explains to me Camilla's heart is atrophying. Dinesh says surgery will not fix it and medicine can only slow its degradation.

It's now clear to me this doctor appointment is really for me. Camilla holds my hand as Dinesh keeps talking. I hear some of his words but I can't hear others, as I'm in and out of the conversation and the room is spinning one way but my senses are heightened and I can feel the earth rotating in the opposite direction. Dinesh says I can expect Camilla to get more and more tired. Camilla squeezes my hand and the room stops spinning. Through all the white noise I hear Camilla say very clearly, "I'm going to be okay, Tommy. Don't worry." Even after everything, my mother still comforts me.

———

At first, I struggle to open the door to exit the hospital. Then the gale pushes it wide open. Camilla takes my hand as we trek out into the wind tunnel. The gust pushes us with such force that we teeter forward and then lurch back for fear of being toppled over. We make it together to the end of the tunnel and suddenly we are out of the wind. Camilla and I look at each other as if we've just survived a grave battle. My family is made up of survivors of disasters, natural or otherwise. From Camilla's eyes, I can tell she's tired so we take the journey to the parking spot slowly, one step at a time. I savor this intimacy with my mother as she holds me close and we walk together.

We make it to the parking lot and are about ten yards from Camilla's Saturn. Mom asks me to pause for a moment. She needs to gather her breath. I oblige. As we rest, I watch a woman walking toward us talking at her cell like it's on speaker-phone. She's sharply dressed. The woman wears tights and boots, and a long puffy coat with fake fur trim along the hood. I assume she's walking toward the hospital entrance. If anything, she strikes me as a loud talker and a bit of an attention seeker. Plenty of people are like that these days. This mid-age, marginally attractive woman reminds me of ten thousand others who have walked right by me whether in Los Angeles or Buffalo. As she draws close, I see the wildness in her eyes and realize her put-together wardrobe is merely a disguise to cover her insanity.

The woman stops right in front of Camilla aggressively. "You stole from me bitch!" she shouts. You stole from my family!" Before I can react, the crazy woman waves a hand in Camilla's face like she's going to slap her. The lady's hand's so close I can see brightly painted magenta nails. She pulls her hand back at the last instant.

I step between the crazy lady and Camilla. "Get out of here!" I shout.

"You get the fuck out of here!" she retorts.

"Can't you see she's sick?"

"We're all sick! She's a liar! She took everything!"

Camilla tears up at being called a liar, "It's okay, honey. I'm sorry for everything."

I stare at Camilla, shocked. How can she be so benevolent at a time like this? If Frank were here, he would have taken this bitch's head off.

"Damn right, you're sorry!" the crazy woman bites back at Camilla's kindness.

"Get the fuck out of here!" I scream as a gob of enraged spit flies from my mouth and I watch it descend all the way to earth like a grotesque falling comet.

"We're all sick!" the crazy woman shouts one last time at both of us as she hustles away.

Camilla and I look at each other. I see in her eyes this crazy woman's words have hurt her beyond this moment. What was Camilla really apologizing for back there?

You wouldn't think there'd be a lot of subtext in an Italian American family. Yes, there was lots of loud talking and epic gesticulation. Yes, there was screaming and the occasional slap if you were out of line. Yes, there were feelings constantly flying around the room and often sticking to the lampshades or walls and hanging there ever-ready for the next dramatic outburst. But there was subtext, too. There were the big things masked in other little things. Then, of course, there was the biggest thing that was never implied at all. Because some things you just don't dare touch. I don't know what Camilla was apologizing for back there, but it strikes me as something buried deep in our family's past. In an attempt to shut out the lingering question in my mind, I slam the door. Asking about the subtext of the apology is not an option. I'm afraid of what Camilla's answer might be.

ELEVEN
THE BUFFALO NEWS

The next few days pass by like lame little soldiers. We all do our duty around the D'Angelo residency. I dote on Camilla and she allows it. It worries me to tangibly realize how much her tired, old heart is troubling her, and how little I can do to give her a reprieve. If I could let my heart do some of her pumping, I would. But that's not how it works.

Speaking of tired old things, The Buffalo News is the only newspaper in Buffalo. Warren Buffett's Berkshire Hathaway has owned it for some time. It has no competition, not anymore. There used to be another newspaper, The Buffalo Courier-Express. They coexisted together for years on a gentleman's agreement. The Buffalo Courier-Express covered the morning paper and The Buffalo News (then called The Buffalo Evening News), the evening. The Buffalo Courier-Express closed up shop in 1982, a couple of years after I was born at Sisters Hospital. I don't take any personal responsibility for its closing. The local newspaper guild blocked a deal to sell the paper to Rupert Murdoch's News Corp and that was the end of the Courier-Express. Good for them. Fuck Rupert.

Can you imagine a world where newspapers were owned by actual people, and not huge monolithic corporations? It existed, in Buffalo, and not terribly long ago. Mark Twain was part owner of the Buffalo Express, an earlier iteration of the Courier-Express. That's right, Samuel Langhorne Fucking Clemens. He might be the very last American to actually have a heartbeat. He died in 1910.

The great concern of our time is there are less obvious dictators. Can you stab corporate bylaws in their blackened heart? Like religion, we learn from corporations how to live because their stories are simple enough and we are too lazy to teach ourselves our own morality. Corporate religion says to take it all and to take it quick. Fuck hard and fuck fast and don't bother covering your own ass because before you know it you're gone baby. You are already gone.

My novel about the man who is turning into a wolf isn't going anywhere. As a writer, you stare into the abyss beneath your feet and pretend it's not there. Eventually, you see the great hole because your delusions aren't strong enough. Then you're stuck. People call this writer's block. I've been pretending to write while staring out the bay window for some time. When I do so, I think strange thoughts. What's the turkey up to in the woods? I haven't seen him lately. Should I call Lauren? I don't think so. She hasn't called me since that dinner. It might be best to let sleeping dogs lie. I have no interest in recreating my past relationship failures.

Camilla's taking a nap in her room right now. Sometimes I go in there to see if she's breathing. Creeping in, I put my ear next to her mouth. If I can feel her breath, I know everything is still good in our world. The last time I checked was an hour ago.

I look out the window and watch as a run-down mini-van pulls into Priya and Neel's driveway. There's a large Buffalo News decal on the driver-side door. I guess the newspapers are being dropped off so Neel can deliver them. Whoever's in the van is just sitting there, taking their time getting out. The van's a Dodge Caravan. These vans were around in spades in Cheektowaga in the nineties. Not anymore though. Now most people drive sport utility vehicles. Corporations sell consumers products they don't need by preying upon the one truly inimitable human quality, our vanity. SUVs were sold to soccer moms based upon the premise they deserved vehicles that can do more than cart around their children.

With an SUV, Suburban moms are adventurous; can go anywhere, and they deserve adventure, too, dammit. Why? Because being a soccer mom is hard, especially with all the antidepressants. Being a soccer mom is even harder because their inept husbands' cocks are barely functional despite all their Viagra. Around the same time as the mini-van to SUV turnover, soccer moms were also being sold a bill of goods about their attractiveness. They are hot sexually. Super-hot. In fact, young men can't keep their penises away from them. The media at this time was all MILFS and Desperate Housewives. And that bullshit's still going strong today. I call it the Kim Kardashian phenomena. "The Feminine Mystique" on Molly pills. But having a big ass is not the same as having a Kim-Kardashian-ass. It's having a big fat ass. And the reason our fat asses are so fat in the first place is because we're eating bullshit we don't need. It's not circular reasoning; it's cellulite reasoning.

Out from the Caravan jump four middle-aged white dudes. All of them are overweight but in the dad-body-mode accepted by most men these days. They have beer bellies. Like, don't worry, it's just a beer belly. It's just beer. It'll go away. No problem. Let me clue men in on something here. It's not a beer belly if the fat sits on top of you in the middle of the night like a fifty-pound toddler that's slowly suffocating you.

Like women have been sold their bullshit, men have, too. Men believe their tummies can look like semi-truck tires, but their secretary who just graduated from a for-profit school is wetting her panties thinking about them. Let me assure you gents, she's not. She's thinking about how she can pay off all that loan debt from a school that only afforded her the opportunity to be a secretary at your shitty job and get a man younger than you with a functional cock and without a beer gut. That way, she can more easily locate his appendage for procreation purposes before her eggs dry up.

From a drawer in the end table nearby, I grab my old binoculars. A week ago, I found them under my bed and placed them in the drawer to be ready. Having binoculars nearby to spy on the suspicious happenings in the old neighborhood is way more important these days than a fresh condom in my pocket. Peering through the binoculars, I see a Cheektowaga Police sticker on the rear bumper. Odd. On a pad of paper, I jot down the license plate. I find in an investigation the details are important. Let me rephrase. I found when writing a detective procedural that went unsold that the details were important. That's also probably true in a real investigation. The mid-age white dudes knock at the front door and Neel strolls out. He fidgets with his beanie nervously and then opens up the garage halfway. I can't see in. Out of the back of the van, the white dudes unload a big blue barrel. I'm guessing that's not a barrel full of newspapers.

The middle-aged white dudes carry the barrel into the garage. As they exit, Sal pulls up. The mid-age white dudes fist bump with Sal. They chat for a minute but it all looks very transactional, familiar and not friendly. The white dudes get back in the van and caravan out the driveway and up the street.

Neel reenters the garage. He walks out with a newspaper bag strapped over his shoulder that appears to have some weight to it. But it certainly isn't papers in there – more like a pint-sized paint can or something. Neel ties on a newspaper belt around his waist as he greets Sal. He climbs in the passenger-side of Sal's truck with the newspaper bag around his shoulders. Sal enters his truck, driver-side. By the time I hear the truck door slam shut I have Camilla's car keys in my hand and I'm running to the front door.

I turn on Camilla's car as I watch Sal and Neel drive up the street and around the bend in the road. If there's one other thing I learned in writing and failing to sell that spec detective feature, it's to keep your distance when following but not to be too distant because then you're not following at all. At that point, you're just driving by yourself. Come to think of it, you could apply that shamus-advice to effective intimacy in relationships. I have to write that metaphor down when I have the chance. In relationships, like following your degenerate cousin and Indian teenager paperboy, you want to be close, but not too close. You want to be distant but not overly so. That's the intimacy balance that drives women crazy and keeps them wanting more.

My problem with women is I've always been off in the intimacy ratio. I've either been too near or too far away. Camilla and Frank are to blame. Mom was too close and Dad was too far. You see, my earlier colossal the-entire-city-is-on-fire relationship failures were not really my fault. I never learned the right way. That's on my parents mostly, even though Frank is long dead and Camilla is near dying. Moving forward, it's going to be better, I think. I'm going to keep on having relationships and failing them utterly until I perfect the intimacy equilibrium so the future Mrs. won't leave me or I won't abandon her for fear she will leave me one day.

Sal and Neel turn down Cindy Street and then to Diana Drive. Today is collection day. That's when the newspaper boy, Neel in this case, goes door-to-door and collects from all the consistent customers and deadbeats alike for all the newspapers they bought over the last couple of weeks. I never mentioned this previously, but I was a paperboy when I was Neel's age. Collection day was a pain in the ass. I'd collect like clockwork, every two weeks on a Wednesday. Not everyone would be available when you'd collect, so there would be people who hadn't paid for a couple months or longer.

If the deadbeats didn't pay, it was my responsibility as newspaper boy to cover them. It's not like you could run points on their debt either. And there was no way the Buffalo News wasn't going to get paid. The Buffalo News took the money right out of my pay. Delivering newspapers was a great lesson about money. Everyone is fucking you from the deadbeats to the tycoons, and if you're the weakest, you get jackhammer screwed.

When I'd finally get a hold of one of my deadbeat neighbors, they'd argue with me about the amount they owed. They played the victim, and acted like I, as an all-powerful and coldly calculating fourteen-year-old paperboy, had concocted a diabolical plan to swindle them. Eventually I'd convince most of my deadbeats to pay up, but they sure as shit weren't giving me a tip after I threatened to not deliver to their address anymore. Of course, it was awkward thereafter because it was the neighborhood. Talk about shitting where you eat. As a fourteen-year-old, I may have just had an argument with a neighbor over money, but then she'd be over to the house the following Tuesday to play my mother in pinochle. There's no going back after you confront a deadbeat. Things have been said. She may have been at my house the next Tuesday, but she was the enemy forever. I'd deliver her paper, but I'd keep my eye on her deadbeat ass.

I keenly watch the following…

Sal pulls up curbside on the street. Neel jumps out of the truck without his newspaper bag. He heads to the front door, rings the door bell and waits. At every third house, someone is actually there and pays Neel for the paper. He puts the money in his belt and hoofs back to the car. This is all normal. At the sixth house, things get interesting. Neel walks to the door with his newspaper bag slung around his shoulder. At the door he speaks to a teenage girl. He hands her a baggie of something, but I can't tell what exactly. I'm across the street and dipped low in Camilla's Saturn to avoid being noticed. My binoculars are fairly effective from this position. If I look creepy, I look like many other creepy people in Cheektowaga because I have on my camouflage. On my way out the door, I grabbed one of my father's old Buffalo Bills winter hats so I'd fit in. If you wear a Buffalo Bills hat around here, no one questions you. I could be walking around the neighborhood wagging my dick at old women and no one would think anything of it. Frank's old hat has a red tassel on top of it. I always hated tassels when I was a kid, and it embarrassed the hell out of me that Frank wore this hat religiously. Now, I can live with them. I've evolved on the tassel issue.

The teenage girl hands Neel a wad of cash. He pockets it in his newspaper belt. She recedes into the house and then the door closes. Neel jaunts back to Sal's truck with a lift in his step. He gives Sal one of those upward tilting nods before he gets in the truck. Sal speeds off.

I watch Sal and Neel collect at exactly fifty-three houses. No one was home at fifteen homes. At ten houses, the curious exchange of baggy for wad of cash goes down. After Sal and Neel complete their collections, they stop at McDonald's. Sal gets a coffee or a hot chocolate. It's impossible for me to know for sure, given I'm spying from the Burger King across the street in order to keep my cover. Neel walks out with a to-go bag. It's hefty so I'm betting he has a super-sized meal deal.

Before Sal and Neel make it to the truck, I see Lauren walk out of Burger King. On instinct, I panic. I back out of my parking spot so fast and slam my brakes so hard my tires squeal. Lauren looks in my direction and our eyes meet through my rear-view mirror. I gaze over my shoulder and see Sal and Neel looking over in my direction, too. In my haste, I've made a scene.

Fear makes us do gloriously stupid things. There's no going back at this point. I make a quick turn onto French Road and pull directly in front of a speeding SUV. There's a soccer mom in the car. She's right on my rear bumper, vigorously giving the one finger salute. Soccer Mom speeds past me and cuts me off. She slows down to taunt me. On the back of her SUV, I can read her bumper sticker, "Proud Parent of an Honor Student." Soccer Mom changes to the right lane and lets me pass. She rides my bumper and hassles me all the way down French Road. The entire way she's screaming and gesticulating. I silently mimic her in return. That really pisses her off. She bangs on the roof of her SUV with both hands so I bang on the roof of my car with both hands. She beats her chest so I beat my chest. She follows me all the way to Crabapple Court. I park in Camilla's driveway. Maybe I should be afraid of this lady. Suburbanites are the most drugged-out people in the country. Crack is not our problem, people. It's psychotropic meds given out like candy to people solely with neurotic conditions. By neurotic conditions I mean people who haven't reached their own low expectations and are generally depressed assholes, passive aggressive assholes, or aggressive-aggressive assholes like this lady.

For a second, I think Soccer Mom's going to pull in the driveway behind me and come out shooting. You never know who's packing heat in Western New York. Even Frank kept a hunting rifle. I wonder if it's still around, just in case. The thing is, Frank never hunted. But he could have. People around here not only keep guns around; they're prepared to use them. That fact has made church so much more important in these parts. The Catholics like my mom pray to their saints for safety. But the Evangelicals have made a lot of traction out here since the Jesus movement in the seventies. They sold the fact you can pray directly to the big guy upstairs with their religion. You can see the appeal, especially when you're constantly living in fear. If you cut off the wrong psychotropic-induced desperate housewife or husband around here, getting blasted is a real possibility.

The Soccer Mom stops directly in front of the driveway. I get out of the car and stand between her and Camilla's house, willing to protect my mom and my childhood home if need be. Readiness to do battle is usually enough to avoid it. Sane men rarely want to fight men who will fight back because it's too dangerous. But this woman is not a man, and right now she's not in a sane place. That's not to say she's insane. She's just probably had a very bad day. The Soccer Mom looks me right in the eyes with all her hatred and lays on her horn. I get it, lady. I totally get it. The longer she lays on the horn and throws her eye-knives at me I get it even more. I get it so much I can't help but smile at her in solidarity.

This piercing horn blast is the Soccer Mom's desperate cry to the universe. The walls of Jericho were brought down by such a sound. It's the cry we all have – an outpouring of our collective anguish. The world is unjust. We have rules that don't protect us. They sold us a bill of goods that we're sick, but our drugs don't heal us. The Church is supposed to help, but the clergy abuse us. And all our brightest, shiniest gods, like our SUVs, aren't able to help us out in any sort of tangible way that makes any damn sense. Our SUVs promise us adventure, but they can't even keep us safe from ourselves.

When the thirty seconds are up, the Soccer Mom takes her hand off the horn and lays her head on the steering wheel. Camilla's at the front door at this point. I wave her back inside. Camilla doesn't move. She's never been one to abandon her family in a fight. The Soccer Mom's not moving, and I'm worried. I hope she's okay. After all, I didn't mean to cut her off. Maybe I shouldn't have egged her on. I take a tentative step toward her. Soccer Mom's shoulders start to heave up and down. I stop in my tracks. The heaving continues. I take another step toward her like she's a bomb that could go off at too indelicate of a step. It's tough to do while also avoiding the cracks in the driveway because I've convinced myself if I step on a crack something really fucking terrible is going to happen. This is a neurotic problem not a psychotic one, hence why I refuse to take the psychotropic drugs the doctor suggested.

The Soccer Mom looks up at me as tears stream down her face. I really wish I was Jesus Christ here and could take her in my arms and say we're all sinners and saints really, and not to worry too much because everything will be okay because nothing really matters too much and everything matters so much and that I love her because we might be alive together here in this space. Cutting her off was careless and stupid I'd say, and I only did it because I was afraid and fear is an evolutionary behavior that, in this case, has lost its utility. Evolution is a bitching bastard in that way. We have all these knee-jerk impulses that are totally unhelpful in the now in which we exist. Operating in the present seems important to survival. Someone should give our species that memo.

But I don't say or do anything or move at all. I stay there and rely on another evolutionary instinct – do nothing and hope the danger passes. The Soccer Mom stares straight at me. She wipes the tears gracefully from her face like a queen might if you ever have the opportunity to catch one crying. Soccer Mom tilts her head a little apologetically and runs her hand through her tall hair-sprayed hair. I raise my hand a little like a bishop might and offer an apologetic blessing. She drives down the street and parks in a driveway five houses over.

I guess we're neighbors.

TWELVE

SICK DOG

It's the damnedest thing how a person can be blindsided by something with the highest probability to occur. I should have known it was coming. Prior experience dictated it. Living in reality could have helped my readiness. Unfortunately, these days I'm having trouble deciphering between the real and everything else that I'll call... the otherwise. It's that time of the evening when it's too late to do anything meaningful, so all you do is sit around and think. And I am sitting around contemplating all the latest happenings – all that Camilla's Pakistani doctor told me, the happenings with the Buffalo News and Sal and Neel, my awkward encounter with naked Priya, and my on-and-off again conversation with a wild turkey from the fields who I think might honestly be my spirit guide or best friend or psychologist.

I had a psychologist once who said seeing a therapist is a lot like friendship. At the time, I thought to myself it was better. Friendship has so many unclear rules. The one clear rule that seems to hold up is you can't have sex with your friends. I mean, you certainly can commit the act. But once you do, there's no more friendship because you've crossed a threshold to something else.

Yoga is the most suspicious of activities. I generally assume one takes a yoga class to pass gas socially while staring at other people's asses. My suspicion about yoga didn't stop me from taking a class back in LA, becoming friends with the instructor, and sleeping with her as soon as she gave the green-light. Afterward, I lost a friend but gained a "relationship." After the relationship ended, because she moved back to Illinois to go to graduate school, I lost the relationship and my yoga instructor. I prefer psychologists to friends. The boundary is crystal clear. I pay them an hourly rate for something akin to friendship. They don't have to be available when I'm not paying them, but I do expect them to be engaged during our allotted appointments.

The wild turkey is more like a friend than a psychologist. I don't know the rules of our relationship, but I haven't talked to him for a few days and, for some reason, that concerns me. My cell rings and I pick it up on autopilot without looking at the ID.

"It's Otis," Lauren says. "I think he's dying."

"I'm sorry to hear that." And I truly am sorry to hear about Otis. Sometimes I feel so cold with people, but not with dogs. It scares me a little that if Lauren would have said her dad was dying I think it would've probably bothered me less than hearing about Otis. My eyes tear up.

"I need to take him to the vet," Lauren says. "But he can't move. My father's back is out and my mom and I can't manage to get him into the car. I'm sorry to bother you. I just... I just felt like I should call you... like you'd know what to do."

She's right. I know exactly what we have to do. Otis is a loyal dog, and it's our job to see this through until the end.

"I'll be right over."

Pulling into Lauren's parents' driveway, my mind is clear and I'm steady for what feels like the first time in a long time. I walk up to the front door. Lauren greets me somberly. Her eyes are puffy. It's obvious she's been crying, but she's more attractive to me now than ever. Lauren guides me to the living room. Otis is in the middle of the space. Lauren's dad and mom are there, too, surrounding him on each side. I look over and see that someone's lit a candle on the end table nearby. The lighting of this scene reminds me of the church I went to as a child. Lauren's parents greet me somberly and shake my hand. Her dad speaks and his voice cracks as he looks up from Otis into my eyes, "He's a good dog."

I bend down and put my hand gently on Otis's side. "You're tired, boy. Aren't you?" Otis looks up at me with his big pure brown eyes with sadness and pain and I can feel his spirit inside me as our ancestors must have run together in the same pack many years ago. Back then, I was his father and he was my son or he was my father and I was his son, or maybe we were brothers. In his eyes are all the universes of everything and nothing that ever never mattered.

"I'll lift him up myself. It'll be easier that way." I pick Otis up in my arms. He makes a low rumble that is more a soft plea than a sign of his discontent. That's right, boy. You're a good dog. You never complain, though you are certainly entitled to. I suppose that's true for people, too. The ones who have the most right to complain seldom do. Then there are the spoon-fed others who have everything lined up for them since birth. They always find a reason to complain. It's a caviar-isn't-fresh-enough type of thing. But Otis isn't that sort of rich miscreant. His richness comes from a pure life, well lived, and replete with love of the good things, smelling asses, eating anything and everything edible or not, and taking care of one's family no matter who they are or what the cost. We need more people like Otis. Even the ass smelling thing can be useful. At least that way people would know what stinks – is it their own ass or the poodle-looking dude next to them?

I cradle Otis's weight against my chest and prop up his head between my bicep and shoulder because he's too weak to keep it up on his own. Lauren and her parents look at me with concern. They're afraid I can't manage alone. They're mistaken. They underestimate my capability to complete a task that means something to me. Lauren steps forward to help if need be, but I signal her off with the seriousness in my eyes. I stagger through the living room with Lauren out in front of us leading the way and her parents trailing behind. We must be a motley crew of parade participants to the grand marshal God who is most likely not watching us from above. I manage not to bang Otis or myself on any of the furniture. The three steps to the front door are precarious but I avoid disaster. Lauren steps out in front of us and into the cold to open the storm door. She's not wearing a coat and neither am I. The cold doesn't matter anymore. We are sad, yes, but the clear purpose that comes from knowing what's right for a change and actually doing it is enough to keep us warm. "I'll take him in the Saturn," I offer.

Lauren opens the back door of the car, and I place Otis gently inside. In another context, I imagine Otis would have been quite pleased to take a ride. Lauren's mom touches Otis with her hand and whispers goodbye. Lauren's father stretches his hand toward Otis but can't bear to touch him. When he turns away, I see a tear zigzag down his unshaven face. Lauren steps into the backseat and sits beside Otis. I shut the back door and climb into the front. Lauren's parents stand there not knowing what else to do as I back out of the driveway.

Careful not to jostle Otis, I slowly drive down Caroline Street. "I've had Otis since he was nine weeks old," Lauren's voice cracks with emotion. "Can you believe it?"

Looking back, I see Otis rest his head on Lauren's hand.

I carry Otis into the Cheektowaga Veterinary Clinic. Lauren called ahead and the vet is already there to meet us. Otis is so weak his entire body is limp. It's not lost on me that this scene reminds me of a Jesus movie I saw as a child. In the scene I remember, Jesus is dead and one of the apostles is caring his lifeless body to his tomb. The music is swelling in the film, but our only soundtrack at the clinic is the occasional weak bark of a dog in the back room that's recently post-surgery.

Lauren talks to the vet at the front desk. The vet comes out from behind the counter and looks at Otis and then at me knowingly. "Follow me," she directs.

I follow her with Lauren right by my side. The vet opens a door and we enter a large room. "Put him right on the floor," she orders. It doesn't feel right to me to put him on the cold concrete floor, but there is no other option. I lay Otis down on the floor and he grumbles again, but even that is weaker than back at the house.

"He was okay," Lauren explains to the vet. "And then all of a sudden he couldn't move."

"We'll do some tests." The vet draws some blood from Otis who remains motionless.

It's been about an hour, and by this point we're all on the floor together. Otis remains on his side. Lauren and I are holding hands. Each of us has our free hand on Otis. Lauren is holding his paw delicately as one might a small child. My hand is on his back, gently, without applying any weight or pressure. I can feel his breath laboring through my hand. The vet reenters the room. "It's cancer," the vet informs clinically.

"Is there anything we can do?" Lauren asks.

"No. There's nothing." The vet is wearing a sad face like it's a costume she brings out for these occasions. In that way, she reminds me of my old psychologist. He'd always wear his sad face at particularly tough sessions to show he was feeling my suffering. And it wasn't offensive or condescending at all. It was just good vocational training. The same holds true for this vet. It's obvious she's been in this spot many times before, and perfected her response through repetition. "I can put him down for you, if that's what you want."

Lauren looks at me pleadingly, "I don't know what to do."

"Is he suffering?" I ask the vet.

"He's a good dog and can't speak up for himself. He can't move at all, and that tells us enough. It's safe to assume he's in a lot of pain."

"Then it's time," I say.

"Will it hurt?" Lauren asks.

"No, but it will happen pretty fast. He'll get two injections. The first will be a sedative so he'll be relaxed. The second will stop his heart. When I give him the second, he'll go very quickly."

Otis's too tired to look up at us. But he knows we're there and we're talking about him. His awareness is really so much greater than ours. He understands his time is up, and that's something we have a lot harder time dealing with. I gaze in his eyes and then through his eyes into his being and all of a sudden, I'm in his mind and he's remembering being a puppy and laying on Lauren's stomach on her bed. Lauren puts him down on the floor because she's afraid she'll roll over in her sleep and suffocate him. But he whimpers and cries until she puts him on her stomach again. His eyelids close slowly like a camera shutter and the last thing he sees is Lauren fast asleep. Then Otis suddenly smash cuts to running around a backyard garden in the warmth of daylight like a crazed, happy wild-dog. He's chasing a squirrel just to chase a squirrel, but the squirrel thinks he's very serious. The sun is on his back yet he's cool still and every particle in his torso is experiencing absolute unhindered pleasure. The squirrel hops up a fence and then over into an adjacent yard and keeps running through another back yard until Otis can't see him anymore.

While I watch his memory, I hear a "voice over" like I'm in a movie. The voice is gruff like a great grandfather who lived hard and true. "It's okay, Tommy. I've run well. I will rest in the earth and be welcomed like all my brothers and sisters before me. I began this life with gratitude and I end it satisfied. Please, Tommy. Tell Lauren I'm…"

I finish Otis's thought for him out loud, "He's ready. Otis wants you to know that he's ready."

The vet prepares the first syringe and holds up the needle for us to see. "This is the sedative," she says.

Otis doesn't flinch at the injection.

"If you want to say goodbye, now's the time," the vet says as she draws another needle and fills up a second syringe.

Lauren lays her head on Otis's side. On my knees, I position myself so I'm nearly lying down. My elbows keep my chest a couple of inches off the concrete. Otis can see my eyes now. "Goodbye Otis," Lauren stammers out between tears.

The vet looks to me and I nod. Out of my periphery, I can see her find a vein, push in the needle, and press down. There is no sign of pain in Otis's eyes. We look at each other. I don't look away until he's gone. The vet nods at me. I place my hand gently on Lauren's back, "It's over. He's not in pain anymore."

The vet asks us what we plan to do with Otis. She says she can take care of his body for another one hundred and fifty dollars. Lauren asks the vet how they dispose of the body. The vet says they are cremated. The vet isn't being crass here. She's doing her job. Despite appreciating her position, I have a negative, visceral response to her offer to cremate Otis for a hundred and fifty bucks that I bite back on and in so doing actually bite my tongue. So, I'm tasting my own blood when I ask Lauren if she'd like us to bury Otis ourselves. Lauren's okay with that but says she doesn't want to bury him at her parents' home. I tell her I know a good place.

It's not that I have anything against cremation. It's in my will I be cremated someday and my ashes scattered over the Pacific Ocean. My strategy is to leave without a corporeal trace. Why not? If my life didn't matter much while I lived it, I figure it will matter less when I'm gone. That and I don't want my corpse to be buried and eaten away by worms and bugs and whatever else. I want to go out in a blaze of glorious ambivalence. But Otis wanted to be put in the dirt with all his brothers and sisters. That's what he told me, and I plan to honor his wish. Will someone do the same for me after I depart? It's the greatest test of friendship. The dead will never know if we honored their last wishes. But that's all the more reason to do what we've been asked.

It's around 4:00 a.m. but it's still dark out. We're driving. Otis is in the backseat wrapped in a sheet. I hit a huge pothole and his body moves sacrilegiously. The shovels I picked up from Lauren's parents are in the trunk clanging about like perverse church bells. From the front seat, Lauren unstraps her belt. She reaches behind and pushes Otis's lifeless vessel further back on the seat. For a moment, her ass is right in my face and it's sheer damn luck we don't hit the car parked in the road directly in front of us. I swerve a little. Otis's body slides again, but this time Lauren leaves him.

We make it to Crabapple Court. I pull aside where the street dead-ends to the field. Years earlier the developers intended to tear down the fields and create a whole new development. The two homes on either side here would have been the first two homes on the new street. The Crabapple Court residents with homes next to the field bought the land behind their properties to limit any future expansion. It's funny how people are happy to buy homes in a development but as soon as they do, they want to keep others from doing the same damn thing. I guess that's America for you.

Lauren and I exit the car. None of our neighbors are up yet for work. It's that lifeless time in the morning before the sun comes up. I have this sudden feeling everyone is dead and we're the last people alive. But it's not even as if we're alive really. We're just here, more like half-alive or half-dead wandering in a sea of flickering electric lamp lights that barely cut the darkness. This is a familiar feeling for me these dark days.

I pop the trunk, grab the two shovels, and hand them to Lauren. She holds the tools familiarly. Lauren's a woman who has known work, and that's something to be respected. Then I open the back seat and lift out Otis. He's heavy and that somehow seems wrong in my mind. I keep thinking if he's dead he shouldn't have all this weight. But that's not how it works. The life is gone but the body's still here awhile longer. It's like his body hasn't received the message yet that the party is over and it's still holding out hope for life to return. I can see why the idea of resurrection is so appealing to people, because it seems like someone should be able to breathe life right back into Otis.

Lauren follows as I lead us down a small path into the field. The path's been made mostly by kids on their bikes who just kept on riding and fighting down the wild for years. I did my part in my childhood and the kids today in the neighborhood seem to be doing their part, too. Thinking about how all the kids over the years have kept the path clear makes me feel a little better about the future. Kids seem all crazy today with their Molly pills and raves and various confusing technologies and subsequent behaviors, but enough of them keep riding their bikes through the field to keep this path passable.

We make it to that clearing where there are only three gnarly trees nestled together like old sentries on watch huddling close to stay warm. I lay Otis on the ground near the trees so they can watch over him. This is the spot where, as kids, we used to build forts. It's the place where I learned how people could be cruel to others for no damn good reason. But it's also where I learned about building with a common purpose. All of us neighborhood kids built fort after fort in these trees. With each new fort we hoped to better the structural integrity and the aesthetic architecture of the last. Sometimes we succeeded but mostly we failed and that was okay. Why? Because we were always building again and moving forward in our collective pursuit of perfection. I dig my first shovelful in the earth slowly and cast it aside. Then, I pick up the pace as the physical labor that was more a part of my childhood than my adulthood seeps into my bones from my awakening ancestors. It becomes only about the work. Now that I've expanded the hole, Lauren sticks her shovel in and digs along.

There's beauty in working hard toward an objective with other people. That's what Lauren and I are doing here, together, in this spot during this uncertain time of the day that's smack between a very late night and a very early morning. With every moment that passes, the uncertainty sits heavy even though the clocks in our brains tell us the world is moving forward and the night is passing from black to shadow, and the day is inching ever closer. Though we try our best to delude ourselves that time does not exist, all our senses command otherwise. Pay attention, they shout from inside out via the growing synaptic misfires in our minds and our creaky bones. Will our work matter when we are gone? I look at Lauren and she's digging away. She tosses a shovelful of dirt and our eyes catch in the moonlight. Burying Otis certainly matters to her. It matters to me, too. We dig out our uncertainty and our grief and our fear and then we dig some more and I can feel beads of sweat dripping down my face like tears.

Lauren stops digging first and then I do, too, because our

rhythm's been disrupted. It doesn't seem right to dig on without her. I realize why she's stopped. We've dug a hole almost three feet deep and more than wide enough for the task at hand.

I follow Lauren's lead as she bends down next to Otis. Delicately lifting him together, we place him over the pit and then lower him the best we can. Eventually, we have to let go and drop him in. We look at each other and let go at the same time. Otis's body settles a little cockeyed. This is a cockeyed town in a cockeyed country in a cockeyed world. That much is certain.

As the dawn threatens to break, Lauren asks me to hold her, and I do; and I don't mind because time stops as we're burying a friend in the fading moonlight, because that is our duty, and duty matters to both of us.

Lauren and I walk out of the field holding hands. There's a mist crawling along the ground and following us all the way to the station wagon. I open the passenger door and Lauren climbs in. There's a little more light out, but you wouldn't call it morning, yet.

I put both of the shovels in the trunk. The moment I sit in the wagon, Lauren kisses me. I'm a little startled. I pull back.

"Is this okay?" she asks. "I just want to feel something else besides sad."

"Yes. It's okay." I kiss her back and then we kiss deeper and deeper until it's like we are one person connected by our entangled tongues. Does this communion always exist between people, and kissing and fucking allows us to actually feel this reality? If that's the case, then maybe we're orgasming together all the time.

Sex is never like the movies. On camera, a couple looks at each other. Then she smiles or he smirks to give an indication something sexy is happening under the surface between them. The better directors allow that subtext to be shown only in their eyes. But, nine times out of ten, there is a sharp cut to passionate totally un-awkward male dominated "love-making" that's more like a dance than a carnal act.

Of course, in real life, we don't really make love. We fuck, because we're animals, and animals fuck. And, it's obvious to anyone who has ever had sex, no one party is ever solely in charge of the endeavor. Yes, we have the little dominant-submissive games we play if those are the games we're into. But there are lots of games to play. And even as the games are played, the rules are more animal rules. That scares some people. It never has me.

Lauren takes off her own shirt and helps me with mine. This is never going to work in the front seat and we both realize it simultaneously. Lauren crawls in the back and I follow her. She removes her jeans by lying on her back and sliding them off. Damn, she's good at taking her clothes off. I don't find her ease at doing so in any way alarming. In fact, I find it encouraging. We need more space so I collapse the back seats. I push the clanging shovels back as Lauren unzips my jeans. They're really hard to take off. I wish I wasn't so goddamn fashionable and my jeans weren't so tight. Lauren pushes me back a little aggressively and I bang the back of my head on the window.

"Sorry," she whispers.

I don't dare respond as she tugs and pulls and takes off the first leg of my jeans. The second leg is even more difficult than the first. Finally, Lauren grunts as she makes one last animalistic pull. The jeans soar off and fly into the front seat. The force of Lauren's last pull is so strong that she bashes her hand on the window behind her. "Shit!"

"Are you okay?" I ask from my rather vulnerable position. My legs are spread eagle. Lauren looks between my legs and sees my favorite appendage completely erect and staring right at her. The look in her eye is unlike any I've ever seen from a woman before. It's pure animal desire. She swoops down and puts me in her mouth.

Lauren blows me without any hint of reservation. For the first time in forever, I have no thoughts. I am present. I am relaxed. After a minute, she stops and looks at me. She leans with her back against the window and spreads her legs.

Lauren is vulnerability. She is beauty. I go down on her licking and kissing. Relaxation. Pleasure. Peace. I repeat this meditation in my mind with every kiss and probe with my tongue. Lauren touches my head and lifts it up. She leans me back and climbs on top. Lauren puts me inside her and rides me like I am a bull at a country western bar, slowly at first, and then with increasing vigor. I have never felt so taken care of in my life. She climbs off and I move on top of her without saying a word. I ride her through this new territory with an ease that somehow feels familiar. Maybe I've lived this life before in a strange dream. I ride and ride with no concern for the culmination or whether it will come too soon.

Lauren whispers something and I can't quite hear her.

"What?" I say.

She's louder this time, "I want to do it from behind."

I back off of her and she pivots around, presenting herself on all fours. I enter her. For a few thrusts her head is hitting one of the shovels. She's so into it, it doesn't bother her at first. Lauren knocks the shovel with her hand. I cum inside her and she screams in pleasure. For a moment, her voice sounds like a howl. Then, I wonder if that sound is me and I'm howling, too. I think I am.

The porch light is still on at Lauren's parents' house. She's about to get out of the car. We're delaying the inevitable because both of us want to hold onto the intimacy we achieved post-burial. It's definitely morning now. One of the neighbors exits his home, lumbers into his car, and drives off to work. Forgetting this evening's sad circumstances, and the requisite guilt that comes from neurotically fearing forgetting a dear friend's death, and what that means about the friendship, and more importantly what it means about me and my capacity to move on despite experiencing loss, it almost feels like Lauren and I are in high school again. It feels as though the neighbor just caught us because we've been out all night together despite the fact Lauren was supposed to be home by her curfew.

My interaction with Lauren is not that awkward considering we've just been as intimate and vulnerable and utterly physical as two people can be, but that time has passed. Now, we're still pretty close in the aftermath but not as near each other as we were before. With each moment, it's as if we take another small step away from that animal-oneness we experienced. Lauren touches my leg to draw me back. In return, I touch the side of her face and brush back a tuft of hair that's dared to conceal her. But the slow march continues and heightens the distance between us. I can't help but think it'd be nice if the intimacy between people wasn't so damned fleeting. We chase that intimacy like the shadows of ghosts who have haunted us our entire lives.

"Thank you for everything," Lauren says. "I couldn't have done this without you."

"Thank you." And the moment I say it I wish I didn't. I don't even know why I said it. Coming out of my mouth, it didn't feel like an automatic response. It felt sincere.

"Why are you thanking me?"

I take a moment to think and the moment swells and gets so fat I'm afraid it's about to blow out the windows like a tremendous shattering fart that's been suppressed for a long first date and then suddenly, violently released.

"For trusting me," I stammer.

Lauren smiles and kisses me softy on the lips. "Good night."

Before I can say good night, she's already exited the car and I hear the door close.

Lauren walks into the house. Then I see a sliver of myself in shadow exit through my rib cage and follow her inside. Am I hallucinating again? I wonder if this is what happens with everyone we're intimate with. Do our dark little sliver souls trail them forever? Are those we've been intimate with trying to lose us in the dark as they run across the street before a car comes, or when we get a little lost do they slow down and wait for us and pick us up and carry us like children and coo to us when we are afraid?

I then think of my ex-wife, the one who juggles knives while wearing finely pressed skirt suits as she does cartwheels at her corporate office, and consider the horrific possibility her sliver-shadow-self's been following me all this time.

THIRTEEN

MYSTERIES OF THE COLOSSALLY STUPID

The thing I'm about to do is colossally stupid. It will come back to haunt me, I'm sure. Yet I feel as though I must write Priya a letter further explaining the reasons why I ran from her house when she presented herself naked to me. I'd like to say I made this decision to write the letter from a place of stress. There's truth to that explanation. My mother's dying for one. Her heart's deteriorating and no one knows why. All we know is it's only a relatively short period of time before her heart gives out and her song is over.

I think my cousin Sal is dealing drugs with Priya's brother, for two. Enough said on that account.

Three, I'm fairly confident that by this point I am occasionally becoming a wolf during the night. I'm also starting to wonder how much this wolf-thing is affecting my thought process during the day; either my senses are increasing exponentially to the point where I can sense slivers of souls or I'm hallucinating.

Four, I talk to a wild turkey who may or may not be in my mind, and I feel lonely when I don't see him.

Five, I buried Lauren's dog, Otis. The dog was one of my favorite people in this town, so that's pretty damn sad.

Six, burying Otis brought Lauren and I much closer together, where before we were pulling apart. But being close to Lauren is incredibly frightening. I haven't felt this close to a woman since my ex-wife whose best quality is she's a dart throwing, flip-flop wearing, shark tank living, skulking assassin.

So, it's true I'm a little stressed. It's also true I empathize with Priya. She's a confused person and I can relate. But it's even truer I hate to be misunderstood. I like to blame Camilla and Frank for not being great listeners when I was a kid. Clarifying my position is not, by itself, such a bad thing. The efforts to which I will go to be understood have caused me a world of pain, however. I think writing a letter is a good idea because it's better to be precise in these situations with words and at a safe distance when delivering them.

Hi Priya,

I want to write you this letter to apologize for my incoherent babbling a few nights ago. If I was shouting, that was not my intention. Sometimes when I'm nervous my voice rises involuntarily. It runs in the family. My father was the same way. Given the circumstance of you disrobing, I was in a state of shock. I want to convey to you in clear terms that you did nothing wrong. If I was in a different place in my life and you were in a different place, I assure you I would have responded differently to your offer. Even then, that's not to say anything of a sexual nature would have definitely happened between us. Why? Let's say for sake of hypothetical circumstance, I was

seventeen and you were seventeen, too. Given that hypothetical and an offer of some sexual activity was actually made; given let's say we knew each other about the same amount that you and I actually know each other in reality, which is to say, not very much, I may not have accepted said offer on account of wanting to show you that I respect you.

It's been my experience that people who offer sex right away often want to be loved even though they may think they only want sex, and sometimes offer sex as an unconscious attempt to get love. In my experience, typically, the exchange doesn't work that way. People might accept sex but that doesn't mean they'll give love back. Life is complicated and hard to figure out. Sometimes we think we want sex, when we actually want to be loved, but really need to love ourselves. Figuring out how to love oneself involves daily practice. Saying the words "I love myself because I am worthy of love" can be a helpful daily practice I've found.

In any case, I encourage you to expect respect from the people you allow into your life – your sacred spaces. And I don't mean sacred here with any repressive or puritanical intention or suggestion concerning your genitalia. I simply say sacred in the sense that I believe all of us are animals with sort of angel bits in us. Let's call that a capacity for reason, and that ability makes us valuable simply because we exist. Given the above hypothetical concerning us being the same age of seventeen, I may have also not accepted an offer of sexual activity because perhaps I'd want to get to know you better first and deepen our intimacy before engaging in anything on that level. Again, I wish to reiterate that what I am saying here is based solely on the hypothetical that we are the same age of seventeen.

I hope this letter finds you well and that the awkwardness that occurred between us will allow us to be better distant friends who respect each other's boundaries, but know that from those boundaries and an age-appropriate and legal distance, we care about each other's welfare.

Sincerely,
    Tommy

P.s. I don't mean any of the above with any sort of condescension. I only want to clear the air since you're neighbors with my mom and she holds you in high regard, too. Furthermore, I've made a lot of mistakes in my life. If anything I can say or do can help you to make better choices, I thought it was worth trying to share a little. Also, if there is anything untoward and illegal that my cousin Sal is doing along with Neel, feel free to let me or another adult know what is going on. That sort of contact is appropriate for us to have. I'm sure Neel is a good kid like you, and I wish both of you the very best futures.

It's a little after lunch so I figure this as good a time as any to drop off my letter to Priya. I'm guessing no one is home since school is in session. To support that deduction, I haven't noticed any activity as I wrote the letter for the last three hours from my writing nook by the bay window. I suppose at some point I should actually get around to writing my novel about the guy who is afraid he's turning into a wolf. The narrative's been hitting a little too close to home these days.

Wearing my dad's old Bills' hat as camo, I step outside. A wiry elderly neighbor across the way speed walks his rambunctious Labradoodle down the middle of the street. I wave to him. He talks loudly to himself. "We're not gonna be fat bastards, are we Abby?" Apparently, the dog's name is Abby, though I can't be sure if that's who he's speaking to. This sinewy old neighbor strikes me as clinically insane, but who am I to diagnosis him, at least at this distance. I suppose he's not in a position either to judge me for delivering a letter, let's call it a letter of clarification, to a seventeen-year-old girl. And yet his possible judgment somehow concerns me.

Maybe he reminds me a little of my father, Frank. They certainly have a similar build. These are the sorts of ghosts that really haunt us – the doppelgängers of those deceased few whose opinions we always claimed not to care about at all but still care the very most about, even in their absence. By the time I make it down the driveway and turn toward Priya's house, he is nearly out of sight as he turns up the block.

I speed walk up the sidewalk like my dead father's doppelgänger and into Priya's driveway. Touching someone else's mailbox always feels a bit creepy, but I place the letter inside it anyway. Halfway down the driveway, something makes me stop. I'd like to say it was a sound from inside the garage. But, in truth, that would be a lie. The only thing I heard was my own curiosity, and its sound deafened that still voice we all have that keeps us safe, that religious people say is God but is actually our evolutionary instinct to survive.

On impulse, I look both ways and, seeing no one in sight, place my hand on the garage door handle and give it a little lift. It's unlocked. Oh, my goodness gracious, it's unlocked. Why did my brain just turn into Camilla's voice there? I've never even thought the words "goodness gracious" before. I'm starting to wonder if Camilla's voice is my conscience, and that's why I previously spent so much time avoiding my actual real-life mother. That thought makes me a bit sad, but not sad enough not to open the garage door quickly, enter, and shut it behind me.

It's dark but for a sliver of light creeping in from the space between the garage door and the floor. I stumble in the dark searching for the light. Yes, I am aware the above is an overwrought metaphor for life and my oddball life in particular. That said, it doesn't make it any less true.

Ouch! I smack my knee on something hard. Bending too quickly to check the damage, I bang my mouth on the very same thing. It tastes metallic. I believe I'm also tasting a little of my own blood as I bring my hand to my face to touch the impact and stifle a pained scream. Though I don't know what object has caused my suffering, I silently curse its existence. It's the "Allegory of the Cave" all over again. Why does everything in my life always come back to that damned cave?" Plato wrote, "the truth would be literally nothing but the shadows of the images." That guy was a smart bastard.

Something from above smacks against my face and I recognize it as a chain to an overhead light. I try to grasp it and it keeps slipping out of my reach. This reminds me of another experience I've tried to put in the past – the dark years when I tried to hold onto a marriage that was already over but I just didn't know it yet. For a moment, this neurotic fear comes over me that someone is in here with me, watching with night goggle vision glasses, and noiselessly laughing his ass off. I consider making my way back to the entrance of the garage, but now I don't know where I am and I'm worried about encountering that metal thing again and doing even greater carnage to myself. In one last desperate attempt at the chain, I stretch out and, eureka, catch it. I tug the chain and the light comes on. My eyes slowly get used to the light and I see...

The metal workbench which kicked my ass and, on top of it, what appears to be some sort of laboratory. I see a variety of beakers, petri dishes, and other scientific items I cannot name. To be honest, chemistry class destroyed my GPA junior year of high school. The subject never interested me. It always reminded me a little of religion in the sense we were told by our teacher to have faith in the equations he shared with us. He also was a devout Evangelical Christian so that may have had something to do with his teaching methodology.

In the far corner of the garage, I also see the blue barrel that was delivered in the Buffalo News van. I don't dare open it up because I'm convinced if I touch anything it is likely to blow up. Cooking drugs is not an area of expertise, but I do read the paper and wrote one action spec where my detective lead had to take down a drug lab. These places always seem to blow up when I read about them in the paper, so I made my drug lab blow up in the script – ka boom! In the business, we call that a set piece. So, I'm treading lightly as I check out this lab. I do, however, snap pictures of everything on my phone.

The sound of a vehicle braking outside the house catches my attention. This noise is familiar. It's a school bus. Priya gets rides to school from the Polish kid whose family owns the French Lounge so it must be Neel! I shut off the light.

What do you do when a teenage, science nerd, drug maker is likely to kill you? I freeze. Instead of the garage door, I hear the front door open and Neel's voice. He's talking to someone, maybe on the phone. I can't make out what he's saying. His footsteps plod deeper into the house. Making my move, I run to the garage door, lift it up, and exit. Out of sheer nerves, I accidentally let it drop and it slams shut.

I haul ass out of the driveway, jump Priya's neighbor's fence, and hide under the wooden deck attached to their house. Their little dog who's tied up to a tree in the backyard catches sight of me and barks his head off. I run through the yard and hop the fence into Camilla's back yard. In a full out sprint, I run toward the sliding glass door. Like a cartoon character, I try to slam the brakes but can't and plow right into it.

It's locked.

I run around the house. Peering around the corner, I see no one is out and about. I make it to the front door and reenter, safely at home.

Breathe. Breathe. Try to breathe.

FOURTEEN

THE END

"Mom!" I shout. She must be out. But her car is in in the driveway. Maybe she walked to the corner store or something. Finally, I am safe at home.

Damn, my calf feels tight. Take one mental note: need to run more. Also, should stretch more. That's two mental notes, I guess. My entire family is inflexible. Frank couldn't touch his toes either. Take a third mental note: physical inflexibility suggests mental pigheadedness. Address this issue in the near future.

"Tommy" I hear. It's Mom. But she sounds distant. "Tommy," she calls again. I follow her voice to the kitchen. She's not there.

"Mom! Where are you?"

"Somewhere over the rainbow," she faintly sings. Frantically, I run upstairs and search her bedroom, my bedroom, and then the bathroom.

I find her in the spare bedroom. That's the room that was to be for the other son or daughter she was never able to bring into the world. The entire time I've been home, I haven't seen her go into the room once. Yet there she is lying on the floor. She seems like she's asleep except her body rests strangely. Her torso is face down but her legs are bent and a little off to the side. She must have made it down to her knees before she collapsed and toppled over.

Dropping down on all fours, I shake her even though I know she's already gone. My heart explodes into a million pieces that fly out from my chest and make a mess.

I take the cell out of my pocket on autopilot and place a call. "Audrey, Mom is dead."

"We'll be right over, baby," she says.

The phone falls to the floor.

Everyone always told me not to cry. Tears stream down my cheeks. I wipe some away, but it's no use. A few fall on Mom.

Audrey's on the phone and Sal's sitting next to me on the couch. His hand is on my shoulder. Audrey paces in front of us. She knows what to do.

"The doctor said she had a heart attack, T. Call Spider for me please. I'll ring you back as soon as I know more. He thinks it was fast. Not much pain."

I let out a sob. She was hurting. I could tell by the look on her face when I found her. If only I'd been there, instead of fucking around doing stupid shit. Maybe I could have helped her. Or at least just have been there at the end to hold her hand and say I loved her. Everything I cared about before seems so meaningless now. Worrying about a teenage girl. Stressing over my drug-dealing cousin. And here this drug dealer is, taking care of me. Now we have a bigger problem than teenage girls and drug dealing. My dear mother is gone. There's no solution to that problem. No neurotic fixation will keep this new reality at bay.

The visitation Audrey set up is in thirty minutes. We should have left already. No one can see me like this. I'm sitting on the bathroom toilet, sobbing.

When I was four years old, a neighborhood dad hit me in the face with a baseball. Frank was working and some of the older kids convinced one of the neighborhood dads, who was out of a job, to pitch to us for batting practice. Not wanting to be left out, I demanded I be able to play, too. At bat, I leaned in for a big swing but too damn far. The hardball hit me squarely on my nose. There was blood everywhere. I cried because it fucking hurt. The dad took me in his arms and clogged my bloody nose with his dirty white t-shirt. He told me not to cry. I tried my best to stop my tears, but couldn't.

It fucking hurts now and I'm trying not to cry, but I can't stop now either.

"Tommy!" Audrey screams from downstairs. "We've got to go, baby!"

I get off the toilet and step in front of the mirror. My eyes are so puffy it looks like I've been someone's punching bag. Sal's cheap suit is too damn small. My father's fedora needs straightening but I keep it a little cockeyed. I take Camilla's rosary out of my pocket, bring it to my lips, and give it a kiss.

Amigone Funeral Home is a classy establishment in Buffalo for funeral services. There was an old, bad joke among us pre-teens about the place, however. We'd yell to each other, "Am I gone yet?" as we raced our bikes past the place on our way to the baseball park nearby. Sal was with us sometimes.

"Not yet," we'd shout while spitting sunflower seeds out of our mouths just because we could. For us neighborhood sandlot baseball players, sunflower seeds were a step down from chewing tobacco, but a step up from the Big League Chew gum that looked like chewing tobacco. We loved sunflower seeds because eating them, and spitting them out, made us feel more like adults. To us, there was nothing more adult than practicing a bad habit that also included littering while joking about death.

We're only doing a one-day visitation at Amigone. Two days are overkill. Next to Camilla's casket, I'm posted up so everyone can offer their condolences. There is a big line at this point. Sal stands beside me, just like when we were kids.

He whispers in my ear, "I know that you saw some things at the Indian's place. I don't want to say nothing now out of respect for your mother, but things are more complicated than they seem." Sal gives me a showy embrace and struts off.

Numb, I look to Camilla for an answer to a question I don't even know to ask. My mother is wearing a violet dress. That was her favorite color. People often say odd things about the dead at funerals. Usually, it is about their appearance. They say something like, "She looks good." Or they'll try to go a little deeper and say, "She looks at peace." If looks ever mattered, they probably matter the least right now. Even if the person uttering nonsense is trying to pay the bereaved a compliment for taking care of their deceased loved one's decaying corpse, one, I didn't embalm her myself and, two, making sure your dead loved one is presentable for public viewing is a pretty low bar for a display of love.

I turn away from Camilla for a moment and look over and see Audrey and Sal buzzing around the place. Each of them is taking care of everything in their own way. My instinct was correct about Audrey. She's great in a crisis. It's not so much that Audrey comes off as loving drama. She's more like a triage nurse who's at her best when the blood is squirting up high onto the ceiling. In that way, Audrey's the total opposite of Camilla. Mom loved drama, but she's not one you'd want in a foxhole. She'd want to be there, don't get me wrong, even if part of it was to tell the story about the battle later. But the greater part is Camilla was loyal.

Camilla was... Camilla is... My mom has always been loyal to a fault and never understood other's failures in that arena. Camilla would be in the battle with you, but she also had this amazing capacity to ratchet up stress. In other words, she didn't have great nerves and her nerves seemed to activate other people's nerves in a crisis. They definitely activated mine. One time when I was a kid I told my mom I had a fever. By the end of the conversation, she had convinced us both that I had Polio.

Sal's not cool under pressure like Audrey. He isn't subtle either. He probably also thinks the word subtle is either a small sandwich you can buy at Subway or a badass, mini underwater boat. I can hear Sal from here; mind you he's across the room now, berating the funeral staff about the volume of the music they're playing. "It's too goddamned loud," Sal bellows. "I can't hear myself think around here. Turn it down or I'm gonna turn you down."

My uncles, Uncle T and Spider, are by my side, greeting all the fellow mourners. As fucking weird as my uncles are, I'm glad they're here.

"Do you wanna Tic Tac?" Uncle Spider asks.

For a moment I thought he was going to ask his favorite question, "Do you wanna see my spider bite?" and then show everyone his butt. On instinct, I say no. I've learned to say no to my uncle whenever he asks me anything. My Uncle T nods at Uncle Spider and then at me solemnly. Upholding a respectful front on behalf of the entire family is important to Uncle T.

Spider pours some Tic Tacs into T's opened palm as he mutters goofily like he's saying something profound, "Tic Tacs for T. Tic Tacs for T." Uncle T shakes his head and then grasps the hand of the next mourner.

I have no idea who most of these people are. This guy in front of me says he was a co-worker of Frank's from the old paper mill before it closed down. That was thirty years ago.

The guy says to me, "I didn't know your mother, but I'm sure she was a great lady." That's respect. He wasn't even my father's friend. The man is only his former co-worker at a plant that no longer exists. They raised that place to the ground fifteen years ago. And he never even met my mother. Yet he shows up. I smile at him and say "thank you."

Saying thank you to people when you don't know exactly what else to say is a pretty useful strategy. They usually feel good about whatever they've said when you say thank you in return. Also, if thank you doesn't entirely make sense based upon the previous statement or question, it disorients the other party and they go away confused yet assuming it is their fault since I've been so polite. I should write this down; it's a very useful tidbit. When you're the bereaved, you can get away with a lot and people will chalk it up to grief talking.

A proselytizing church lady offers me, "Your mom's in a better place. She's in heaven."

"Swiss cheese," I respond. The church lady doesn't know what to do. She doesn't know if I am saying something thoughtful about the afterlife or want a sandwich. I really said both things while not saying anything. It's beautiful.

Lauren enters along with her sister Kelly and Kelly's husband, Brian. Lauren's parents are there, too. They are all very solemn. Mr. Townsend shakes my hand and looks into my eyes until he starts sobbing. Mrs. Townsend has to peel his hand from mine to take him away. Despite my initial skepticism, he's a good old dude. I'm glad I didn't write him off. You've got to give a guy a freebee when he's concerned about his daughter. I'm glad I didn't write off any of these people. Boundaries are good, but so are giving people chances to impress you rather than disappoint. Kelly gives me a hug and it's not too weird even though she named her baby after me. Brian shakes my hand and that's not too weird despite the fact his wife named their baby after me.

"How is Michael Thomas?" I ask.

"He's fine. Our neighbor's watching him," Kelly and Brian say almost in unison before they take their leave. Lauren stands by me and leans into my side. I appreciate she doesn't bother trying to say anything.

"Can you stay for a while?" I ask.

"Yes. As long as you need."

———

After two and a half hours, the visitation is almost over. I'm still in front of Camilla's coffin and Lauren remains by my side. She hasn't left me the entire time, and I haven't minded one iota. My ex-wife, the woman who hacky sacks with a sack full of razorblades while screaming the world is unsafe, never made it to my father's funeral. We were married then. To say she never made it is a little too kind. At the time, her reasoning seemed to make sense. She had to close a big deal. When you're grieving, it's hard to have the stamina to convince your spouse to attend your father's funeral.

Neel and Priya enter the room. I didn't think they were coming. In truth, I've been dreading the possibility and hoping they'd just be immature kids with better things to do than to go to their elderly neighbor's visitation. It's a weird thing to discover the younger brother of a seventeen-year-old girl you maybe were fantasizing about runs a drug lab in his garage. Thinking about the night Priya presented herself to me totally nude and offering sex is stranger. I turned her down because, after all the doubts I may have ever had, I am mostly a good man who doesn't want to hurt anyone. Still, it's my fault for having urges. Seeing Priya naked has afflicted me with incredible guilt. I feel culpable because of my thoughts, not my actions.

It's funny. I have these animal thoughts, like instinctually wanting to have sex with an exotic-seeming, voluptuous young woman, like Priya, and then I punish the shit out of myself for having those thoughts; even though I didn't act on those passing thoughts when given the unequivocal opportunity to do so. Of course, Priya's not exotic really – unless one considers our shared hometown of Cheektowaga exceptionally peculiar. When I see Priya now, I barely notice her figure. That's what happens when animal urges mixed with fantasy meet reality, and you're a decent person who has some morality when it comes down to it. I judge myself for the improper lizard thoughts I may have had in the corner of my brain, and feel as though these impure thoughts made Priya offer herself sexually to me. It may also be possible these thoughts made Neel a drug manufacturer and Sal, a drug dealer. This is the problem with my brain. I truly think everything in the world happens because of me. That's tremendous responsibility for a regular person. I wish I were a superhero.

Neel and I make eye contact. He nods at me and seems older and more knowing than I remember him. I wonder if he knows I was in the garage and he's telling me so with his eyes. He and Priya approach. Neel shakes my hand. "Sorry, man."

I parrot "sorry" back which is weird because I'm actually apologizing for seeing Priya naked and for him being a drug maker and for Sal being a drug dealer and for my impure thoughts causing all of it, when in the moment saying sorry means I'm sorry my mom died, too. You'd think I was the fifteen-year-old teenager with poor social skills who is also probably on drugs.

Neel peels off and beelines to Sal. Priya lingers for a moment. There are tears in her eyes. Lauren watches us. I've always had this fear the women I've slept with can read my mind. Priya gives me a hug that is a little awkward. "I'm sorry. You're a great guy." Then she leans in. "Thank you for the letter." She walks off toward her brother and Sal. I look at Lauren. She has questions about Priya, and this will come up later. Lauren looks away from me for a moment and I see her gaping at someone else entering the room. So, I stare too.

Holy fuck, it's Barbara! My ex! Help, someone help! She shouldn't be here! Did I just yell all that? No one is reacting, so I think I'm good. I thought I had it bad with Priya a moment ago. Barbara takes her place in line. I watch helplessly. She's four grievers back. We haven't made eye contact yet because I have not allowed it. I wish I would just black out but I don't. Maybe I can make myself faint. Stop breathing. Stop breathing. Stop fucking breathing!

I can't stop breathing. Perhaps I can fake it and pretend to pass out. That won't work. Barbara might try to give me mouth-to-mouth or something, and then I might throw up and choke on my vomit and die. I think about running the hell out of the room. In a pinch, I'm pretty fast. My cardio is good. I do yoga. Everything can be explained later, right? I don't really have fight or flight when it comes to Barbara. It's more flight or become petrified with fear and hope she goes away. The latter might work. I concentrate and fiercely try to freeze my body as well as the time and space in the entire room. For a second, it's apparently working as my brain allows me to think semi-rational thoughts.

Rational thoughts include: Barbara has horrible taste in clothes; Lauren has a strong survival instinct; and I am scared. Suddenly, Sal slips on a program, stumbles to the floor, and scampers up. Despite my best efforts to freeze reality, it's clear to me I've been the only immobile person in the room the last minute. This means the damn line has moved up and Barbara's now directly in front of me. She's wearing a black suit with ass-tight skinny pants and very tall leopard heels. Barbara always had that gauche look-at-me flare to cover the self-loathing underneath. She pulls me in for a deep hug that lingers too damn long.

"I'm so sorry, Tommy," Barbara whispers grandly in my ear.

I resist the urge to retch and in doing so back away from her grasp, clutching my gut like someone's punched me. It's only then I realize Barbara's not alone. There is an effete man beside her. He looks old to me, though we may be the same age. Her companion is wearing a turtleneck sweater under a suit jacket and looks a little like Rand Paul.

"I'm sorry for your loss," he drawls with a southern accent.

"This is my husband, Evan," Barbara says.

Evan offers his hand and, on autopilot, I shake it. His skin is so soft it's off-putting. He holds onto me for what feels like a very long time. It's as if our hands are shaking in extremely slow motion. Shit! We are actually moving very slow. Who is slowing down time? It can't be me since I already tried and failed miserably. Then I realize Barbara is the one slowing down time. She's uttering some kind of dark, ex-wife, corporate incantation they must have taught her in evil, Sith business school.

Why does she have to be so damned good at everything and evil, too? It seems wrong that being evil gives you super powers. Why can't being a neurotic wolf-man give you powers when you need them? Or your mother dying gives you powers? I realize Barbara's the only one who can move in regular time. She sizes up Lauren and dresses her down with her darting devil eyes. Barbara points at her plump tummy and pats it. She's pregnant! Holy shit balls! Jezebel-Delilah is pregnant with turtle-neck-man's southern spawn! That's why she's come. I knew it couldn't really be about paying respects or trying to rectify past mistakes, however unhelpful to me that would have been. Barbara's come to prove to herself once and for all that she is better than me. She wants to show me she's won.

The funny thing is, I stopped playing her game three years ago. I think of Camilla trying to be cordial to Barbara in this moment and a smile creeps up on my face and stays there. Somehow, I'm able to take control and force existence back into regular time and space. Barbara's stunned and her incantation stops as suddenly as our marriage did. Lauren initiates and shakes Barbara's hand.

"This is Barbara, my ex-wife," I stammer a little because though I'm in more control now, it's kind of a new thing and Barbara still really fucking scares me. Lauren doesn't flinch. I can tell Barbara hates that. Lauren won't play her game either.

"We flew in from Virginia this morning." Barbara grins as she looks more at Lauren than at me. "It seems you have a lot of support. But if you need anything, dear, we're staying at the Hilton by the airport until tomorrow." This is the point I realize Barbara won't look at Camilla. That's because she's afraid. Underneath all the accouterments of plastic wealth and vocational confidence, she's fucking terrified of everything, including my dead mother, including me, including her own self whose knowledge escapes her like a slippery ghost, and including death itself.

"Thank you," I say. "Congratulations to you both." And with that, Barbara glides out of the room on ice skates made with shaving blades of pain and is gone.

Uncle Spider says a little loudly, "That icy little bitch."

"Thank you," I mutter to no one in particular. Lauren squeezes my hand. I squeeze back.

This is my third glass of Wild Turkey bourbon. Lauren nurses her second beside me on the floor in my bedroom. I bought the Wild Turkey on the way home from the visitation because it was Hunter S. Thompson's favorite drink. Why not look to the beverage of my writer-guide for direction through this unknown territory into the never-ending night of trepidation and loneliness? Okay, I've had more than several glasses.

"Mom always wanted to be a movie star and a singer like Judy Garland," I slur.

"Did she have a nice voice?"

"She certainly thought so." Lauren cracks a slight grin, and then I do, too. Does momentary respite from grief mean I'm letting Mom down? It's hard to be good about paradox and juxtaposition and nuance when I'm supposed to be sad because death is certain and final and terrible. "Mom had a lovely voice. That's the way to remember her." We clink glasses; Lauren sips and I gulp.

"I wish I could have met her."

"She would've loved you." Lauren rests her head on my shoulder. "I can't believe she's gone. It's strange. I keep thinking she's just in the other room. Waiting for a reply, I swish the bourbon in my glass. A response from Lauren never comes. She's asleep. That's okay. She deserves rest.

The funeral is tomorrow morning. Audrey and Sal hung around this evening until I finally assured them I was all right and asked them to go home. In fact, I pleaded with them. Lauren's presence allowed them to leave. Audrey and Sal trust her to take care of me. It's amazing how family rallies in a crisis. They rally so hard it's tough to get rid of them. The entire family means well, I think, even Sal. I haven't said a thing to him about Neel and the lab. It all seemed so important before, but I just can't bring myself to give a shit about all that right now.

God, it's hard to go to sleep. In my head, I know I need rest. I haven't had one truly restful night since I've been back home. My petty concerns don't seem to matter much now that Camilla is gone. I know she wouldn't want me to think that way. She'd want me to take care of myself. I drank last night, too. In the movies featuring Italian Americans, they are almost always gangsters who get drunk when bereaved. I'm not a gangster though, nor do I play one in the movies. Writers get the same treatment in popular culture about imbibing. If they're not drinking, they're not writing. I am a writer.

That's right, I'm a writer. And I still feel it in my bones even in this grief and despite the fact every indication in the world tells me I'm not good enough. Fuck the world and fuck death, too. There's fire in my belly tonight like that between words and worlds. Someday I'll write well enough to make Camilla come back from the dead, or I'll write a way to transport myself to whatever world she exists on now. If that's a place called nothingness, then that's fine, too. I'll write myself there. It can't be much different than Los Angeles or Buffalo or any other damn place.

Where has that motherfucker, Oliver, been? If he was a good hallucination, he wouldn't abandon me in this dark hour. My life as a character on a cocktail of drugs, including mescaline, from a Hunter S. Thompson novel would make so much more sense. Who knows if it'd be any more palatable? Drugs can be a bit risky in that regard. We take them not to feel but sometimes they help us feel more deeply, and worse. Ask Hunter S. Thompson.

I cannot sleep anymore. Maybe I'll never be able to sleep again and I'll become a kind of undead wolf man without any past or any future and, more importantly, without any guilt. Perhaps I'll just lay awake in this place forever to hold onto the memory of Mom so she will never die.

There's a dead rabbit at my feet. How the fuck did that get there?

My heart beats loudly yet I hear another beside me. Boom. Boom, Boom! Someone's breathing. There's something breathing behind me. Run, you fuck. I sprint on all fours through briar and muck and jump over boulders and smack my paws on sharp rocks. Never stop sprinting. I rest only when my body can't physically continue because my mind is no longer a hindrance because I have no mind.

Looking back over my shoulder I realize my greatest fear – that I'm the only one here. I didn't know I could look behind myself like that, but I now realize I've been breathing down my own back my entire life,

173

and what I thought was the shadow heartbeat was really my own beating in arrhythmia. My own irregular heartbeat was someone else beside me. Sometimes a friend. Sometimes a lover. Sometimes a stillborn brother or sister wolf who attached itself to my vessel for the journey. Yet it was always me.

It's amazing how important our bodies are, yet they are such a damned mystery. Our bodies are deep oceans worthy of exploration. But I'm not an explorer. I'm an undead wolf man, son-of-a-bitch. This is the spot in the field by the tree fort where I first saw power and evil and learned how fucking dark people can be. Death is a bitch, even in the wild. Living things are real like colorful lights and then they go out forever in shadow and then dust. Their bones are shards of becoming nothingness. The earth swallows everything like a giant stupid bear with a gaping mouth and sharp teeth conquering all with the force of its snapping jaws and the terror of its sinister purpose.

There's no one else here. I am alone in terror and awe and night and the irregular beating of my own overworked heart and the breath of my latest kill that lingers like a holy ghost. "Oliver!" I scream at the clouds that pretend they are my friends.

"Oliver!" I scream at the moon who says she loves me but always goes away when I ask her to stay. "Fuck you, Oliver! Fuck you and death!"

At that, Oliver swoops onto his perch. I show him my fangs. It would be so much better to be a flying un-dead wolf man. If I was, I'd smote Oliver's gobbler face for being like all the others who claim to be friends and then don't show up to your father's funeral. Or even worse. He's more like a turkey who was a friend once and then hurt you terribly so you've built the greatest wall ever to keep her out of your life and then she does finally show up at your mother's funeral only to tell you that she's pregnant with an effeminate southern gentleman's baby. "Bastard-Jezebel flying pig turkey interloper she who abandons cause of all ruin and despair and pain!"

"What's up, bro?" Oliver asks.

"How dare you ask me that, you turkey pig fuck?"

"Wow man, you need to smoke some grass or something. You're tense, bro."

"I hate you with a million fire breathing hates."

"What'd I do? I've just been chilling in the fields trying not to get shot by hunters and shit."

"You missed my mom's funeral, that's what's up," I toss back.

"You might want to sit down," Oliver suggests.

I pace back and forth, and then stand on my hind legs like a man. The balancing act doesn't work for long and I'm back on all fours. "I never sit when I'm told."

"Fine. Have it your way. Stand."

At that, I sit right down and scream, "I have died!"

"You're not dead," Oliver cackles.

"Then I'm a dead undead wolf man, pig turkey bastard."

"I've tried to tell you a million times…"

"We've only talked like three or four times," I correct.

"Have it your way. I've tried to tell you a trillion times infinity that no one ever dies. Death is a big joke. You think it's coming like this bullet that's chasing you your whole life. You try everything to keep the bullet away. First, you try to outrun it. When you get older you throw the sicker and older turkeys at it hoping that will appease. When you're even a little older and slower, you'll trip up your best friends and lovers in hope that their carcasses will take the bullet and it will finally be satisfied. None of it works though, because the bullet is always coming no matter what.

Some fools want to talk about the hunter all damned day and night but they'd be better off to keep on running. No one ever sees the hunter. And she don't give a damn about us. You know why, because she doesn't exist. The only thing that exists is the bullet. Even running from the bullet don't matter because the bullet always gets you right in the ass. But even that don't matter because you never die, you just start running again and there's another bullet coming right toward your asshole.

The real deep shit here is there is no bullet and there are no turkeys. There's no nothing and nothing matters so you just got to let all that shit go, man."

I shower, and then walk into the bedroom wearing only a towel. There's mud all over my jeans, which I carry like a fresh kill, but I don't care. I toss them on the floor, think better of leaving them visible for Lauren to see in the morning, and give them a swift kick under the bed. Thank goodness playing soccer as a kid was good for something. Actually, when I played soccer, I learned a few things.

Primarily, I learned most people are gaping assholes. Your teammates typically pick on the weakest links on the team, your adversaries on the pitch seldom play fair and often don't keep proper hygiene, and your own parents will laugh at you when you get inadvertently kicked in the balls. But I also learned if you want to be a good teammate and not an asshole, you have to be honest with yourself and other people.

I look down at Lauren. There's distance between us. She's done nothing wrong. It's just that moment when you come out of a dream and you're faced with the real world, but consciousness feels gray and remote in contrast to the brilliance of the dream before. Lauren's facing away from me and seems asleep. I drop my towel and climb back into bed, naked, in an effort to feel close to her again. Lauren turns toward me. She isn't asleep after all. The question remains whether it was her intention to appear asleep. If I was deceived, it matters a little whether she did the deceiving or I misperceived and deceived myself. Lauren places her hand on my chest, and looks right into my dead/undead eyes. "Where have you been? I've been really worried."

That's a great question, Lauren. Where have I been? Our entire damn lives we've been lost. I want to tell her about the great bullet and how it's always chasing us, but there is really no bullet and there is really no us either – so we're supposed to let all our fears of death go. That's a lot to try to share and I imagine it could be unsettling to people who are leaning more to the rational side of an irrational existence so I take the easier path. "I couldn't sleep, so I went for a walk."

That's not a lie. It's just not all the information. I don't really have the energy to try to explain my meetings with Oliver. Hell, where would I begin? I could start this way... So, Lauren, I'm a dead/undead raving wolf man and I have this love/hate relationship with a wild turkey named Oliver who I visit on occasion in the fields. Not a great start.

"I get it, honey," Lauren says seemingly without any pretense.

I confess to you I hate being called honey with the passion of a million blazing fire suns. Taking that up with Lauren this moment is unnecessary. She's sincere and that's enough. "Can I hold you?" she asks.

Being held might be a good thing generally, but it's the last thing I want right now. I'd rather jump out the second-floor window and catch my balls on a tree branch on the way down. That said, I say, "Sure." I do so because it seems the easier path.

"That girl, Priya. What letter was she talking about?"

That's where all this is heading, the fake sleeping, the wanting to hold me. Lauren is setting me up for the kill. I am dealing with an expert huntress. Now, she's going for it and I have to plan my next move very carefully or face destruction.

I'm thinking about lying. My overactive brain allows me to think deeply on a thing but it doesn't take too long in a way that arouses suspicion. Normally, I'd just lie my ass off about a young girl presenting herself totally stark naked asking me to ravage her body but somehow lying doesn't seem right in this particular situation. Lauren cares about me, that much is clear. And as fucked up as I might be, I care about her, too. I take a mini-breath and then offer, "Priya is a confused kid. She approached me in a kind of sexual way, and I turned her down. So, I wrote her a letter explaining why."

"What's a sexual way?"

"I went over to her house to check a thing, and then she said she had to check on a thing, and then she came out of the bathroom in a robe, and then all of a sudden she was naked. I should mention I didn't disrobe her or ask her to disrobe."

"What'd you do?"

"I ran the hell out of there screaming like my hair was on fire."

"You're a good guy. Some men wouldn't have responded that way."

"That's what I've been trying to tell people for years, Lauren. I'm a good guy. I just look bad, sound bad, and look like I'm acting badly. But I'm mostly good inside."

Lauren laughs. See, women like me and think I'm funny. I guess that's what got me in trouble with Priya. I'm irresistible in an off-putting let-me-inside-your-soul-to-swim-naked sort of way. "What'd you say in the letter though?" Lauren asks. She's too smart and it's a tad upsetting. She could be a corporate climber like my ex, the pregnant one with the southern baby-daddy and the slippers made of the souls of angels she's eaten. Thankfully, Lauren's not that type. She generally uses her powers to help people.

I get back to answering Lauren's question. "I wrote that I didn't want her to think I thought any less of her. I tried to explain to her lots of things I wish I knew when I was seventeen. I wish someone had done the same thing for me. Maybe it was weird but it made sense at the time." The emotional whirlwind of projections of the past mixed with present suspicions is coming, right? Lauren's ex-husband was, in fact, caught getting blown in a shopping mall parking lot by one of his high school students.

Instead, Lauren responds rather agreeably, "That's really very sweet."

I look right into Lauren's deep brown eyes and search for a sign of a mask covering her true intention. Nothing suggests she's bullshitting me or setting me up further for another emotional hammer to drop. She's being honest here.

Wow, Lauren mostly trusts me. I better take that trust seriously, cherish it, and not fuck it up. Sure, she had a question and she felt she needed to ask it on the early morning before we bury Camilla. Maybe that's a little fucked up and maybe not. Sometimes people have something they need to address, and it can't wait. I get that. My preference is to address stuff that's bothering me when I have the self-awareness I'm being bothered by it.

Lauren's concern and question is okay as long as it gets buried like a bad idea. It's unappealing to re-fuck bad ideas or questions of my character for other people. I'm a firm believer that I'm the only one who gets to neurotically torture myself.

Explaining myself to Lauren is clarifying. I may have had a passing fantasy about a young woman, but I didn't have sex with her. Instead, I wrote her a letter explaining why having sex with her was not good for her, me, or the entire fucking universe. Maybe that's a bit of an odd play. But being odd isn't the same as being a morally bankrupt asshole. In fact, in a corrupt world, it may be our oddities that show we are trying to do things better. So, let's not be too hard on the freaks and weirdoes. They might just be, like me, flawed, yes definitely, but trying to do what's really right for their world.

There's a glimmer of something in Lauren's eyes but I can't quite make it out. Then, she hits me with, "I trust you on everything with Priya. I really do. But what was the thing you had to check on over there in the first place?"

"The thing?" I know very well what she's referring to. Telling her Priya called me and asked me to come over isn't happening. It leaves me too vulnerable. I scratch my leg for a beat as I swim through various answers. The water is very choppy because the wind is blowing up north from my own ass. I tell a lie. "It was something for Camilla. She wanted me to help Neel with his chemistry homework. It's weird, I know… because I suck at chemistry. I told her that. I think Camilla just wanted me to check in on the kids. She was a worrier."

What a stupid lie. It's close enough to the actual truth I could've just gone with that. Camilla did care about Neel and Priya. She did want me to look in on them. Mom practically instructed me to look after them. I told you the water was choppy. The chemistry part of the lie came out, I presume, because my brain is swirling around the huge pink elephant in the neighborhood – a drug lab in Neel's garage.

I couldn't share with Lauren all my suspicions about Sal and Neel's drug dealing; and how the Cheektowaga police are probably in on it too; and how I'm a wild undead/dead wolf man at night and maybe during the day now, too. That's just too much right now to share considering everything else. But that's not why I lied.

The real reason I lied is because I know I went over Priya's house because I allowed myself to become infatuated with a seventeen-year-old girl. I wanted her. My fantasy was for her to disrobe. It was in my brain somewhere, in a crevice of a fold in my lizard brain, so I made it happen. I know it. The world is built by our ideas. Those little bastard, mean slivers in our brains strengthen through constant neurotic thought and then connect together to shape and build the world.

I blame myself for everything that's transpired since I allowed that sliver about wanting Priya to enter my mind. It is my fault for becoming a wild undead/dead wolf man who wandered in the fields when he should have been at home taking care of his dying mother. I'm to blame for Camilla's death.

If I wasn't gallivanting around by day led by my penis and then running around at night on all fours in the fields trying to kill my best friend Oliver, I could have focused on other, better, purer thoughts and used my neurotic brain power to create an alternate ending allowing my dear mother to live forever like an Italian American celebrity actor, singer, goddess.

The funeral service is at Church of the Holy Bells. That's the church us kids used to call, Church of the Holy Balls. Lauren is by my side as we walk in. There are a few people here already waiting for service to begin. Lauren and I walk down the aisle toward the priest beside the pulpit. I'm tired. We should have done all this shit in one day. Since we're a big family, Audrey and my uncles convinced me we needed a long visitation and the funeral the next day. I thought that was a mistake and was right.

Sal and Audrey are already here. Audrey is speaking with the priest. My neck feels hot and I am uncomfortable in this place. It's not that I feel particularly sinful. My guilt is neurotic these days, not religious. The reason I left religion behind is all the lovely architecture built with lies to give unimaginative people power over even less imaginative people. Camilla appreciated religion, even though it provided her little real solace from her pain. So, I'll try to play nice.

Audrey looks at me solemnly. "This is Father Polansky." What the hell? A Polish priest? We couldn't even get an Italian. Dad would have been pissed. Mom would have went along with it.

Like Audrey, the priest has a reverent face. "Your mom was a wonderful lady. She's with the Lord now."

"That's right, Father. My mom was a great lady. I get your perspective completely about the Lord, too. Can you do me a favor though?"

"What's that, my son?"

"My mother was religious. I'm not. I want to respect her wishes to have a mass here. But I don't want any proselytizing."

The priest makes a face like he's just eaten shit. "This is a Catholic mass, my son."

Sal's smirking. Audrey's horrified. I can't tell what Lauren's thinking because she's by my side and I'm focused on Father Polansky.

"I get that, Father. But let's cut the bullshit. I'm not your son. You're not my father. I am my father's son though, and I do love my mother. I'm also the guy paying for this service. So, let's have a nice mass but no proselytizing. You'll do your thing and then I'll do the eulogy and we'll get out of here in a half hour without any hitches. How's that sound?"

Father Polansky moves his mouth, but nothing comes out. I slap him hard on the shoulder to let him know what might come should he disobey my wishes. His vocation will not protect him. I strut over to my seat and park it. When my ass hits the wooden pew, an echo reverberates throughout the entire church.

The pews are pretty full. It's impressive. People really come out for this sort of thing. Camilla finally found her audience in her death. Maybe it'll be the same way for me. Father Polanky's in the middle of his sermon. He started out okay. Polanky just said some nice things about Mom. But I can tell he's gearing up for a big finish.

"Camilla's in a better place now," he bellows. "She was a good Catholic. If you want to be with her someday in Heaven, you should become a Catholic, too." At least that's what I think he's saying, because as soon as I hear him turning the corner from eulogizing Camilla to glorifying the Church, which is to say himself, I stand up. Lauren's comforting hand on my shoulder turns to a desperate claw trying to hold onto my sport coat. Her efforts are to no avail. I pull away; make my way down the pew, and climb over a few parishioners who don't move out of the way quickly enough. Bounding down the aisle, I slip, fall to my knees, and then continue on all fours until I can get upright again. At the pulpit, I see the fear in Father Polansky's eyes.

"That's enough, man. I'm tapping you out!" I shout as Father Polansky clings to the pulpit like a drowning man to a piece of driftwood. Polansky's an old man and I have dead/undead wolf man strength now. I pry his stringy little fingers from the pulpit with one hand while lifting him around the torso with my other arm. Gasps ring out intermittently from the audience. Fuck their outrage. They can huff all they want. This is Camilla's funeral, so it's my funeral. I'm the one who's left here with all these people and all this bullshit. A parishioner steps up to intervene and I show my fangs. From the pew behind, Sal grabs the parishioner by the belt and nonchalantly slings him back into his pew. I nod at Sal.

The congregation looks horrified but I don't give a shit. They're going to get my eulogy whether they like it or not. Here it goes.

"I want to say a few words about my mom. Yes, she was a woman who had faith. She had faith in God and, Father Polansky is right, she had faith in Catholicism, too. But her faith was bigger than religion, and I won't have it reduced to some sort of in-club out-of-the-club institutional bullshit. My mom had faith in her family.

"As some of you may know, Mom wanted me to have brothers and sisters. It didn't work out that way. It's a nice thought to think she's with them somewhere now. I really doubt that's true, at least how Father Polansky conceives it. But who knows? I like to think Mom's energy is still out there and her babies' energies that she could never hold in her hands are out there. And maybe all their energies are somewhere together with my father, and maybe I'll get to join them someday, too.

"Maybe that's spiritual bullshit and just as bad as religious bullshit, but it's a nice thought.

"I want all of you to know that Mom was a star. She dreamed of being a singer/actor, double threat. Death is strange. People live and then they die and that's all we know. When I've been sad in the past, I used to be comforted by the thought that life was a nightmare I could wake up from at any moment. But I was wrong. Life is a dream with some weird parts. That's what Mom taught me all these years, only I'm just now understanding. Even though Mom suffered, she believed a good life was measured not in the reality of our pain but in the quality of our dreams.

"I love you, Mom. Thank you."

A smattering of applause is punctuated by Lauren standing and clapping as loud as she is able.

When you're smack in the middle of Briar Lawn Cemetery, you can see all of its boundaries. There are no huge statues designed by internationally renowned sculptures here like at Forest Lawn Cemetery. There is one penis obelisk, however. A Polish woman bought it after her philanderer husband's death. She had the last laugh.

This is the cemetery for my class of people and my father's family's cemetery. Camilla's family is buried about twenty-five miles away in a small, rural town called Derby where she was raised. It's kind of sad both families aren't buried in the same place.

There was no question as to where Camilla was to be buried. Sure, Frank and Camilla had their rows but there was never any doubt they loved each other. Except, perhaps, the one time I heard Camilla screaming, "I hate you, Frank!" I was nine years old and sitting at the top of the stairs. Camilla and Frank loved hard, fought hard, and hated hard, too. It's an Italian thing. We never forget a grievance. Until the day he died, my father bitched about a snow blower he lent to a neighbor in 1974 that was returned busted. Camilla was the same way. That's how she was with Audrey.

It's funny how Audrey has taken care of everything. Maybe she's trying to make up for some guilt she has or maybe their falling out was overblown. My family has always had a way of coming together. They can be the most dysfunctional sort, but when one of us is really in a pinch everyone will show up ready to kick ass. Look at Sal and me. He may be a drug dealer who corrupts nice Indian kids, but he's here and ready and willing.

I stand in front of the coffin facing my family. Everyone is here including my uncles and Lauren. Father Polansky is off to the side. I scared the shit out of him back at Church of the Holy Balls, so he's agreed not to speak graveside. The coffin is over the grave, ready to enter its final position. I step forward, turn to Father Polansky, and raise both my arms menacingly, my hands as claws like Ozzie Osbourne at a rock show. He sees my fangs and steps back. Sal's right next to him in case he gets any ideas. This is my show now, Polansky. I turn back to my family, grateful to be among such a motley crew of misfits. It's strange to feel so at home. Camilla used to pretend she held a microphone as she sang around the house.

I imagine a microphone in my hands.

"I'm honored to be here with all of my family. Some people may consider us dysfunctional, I'd argue honest. Camilla was an honest person in an honest family that sometimes could be a little too honest. If that's the worst thing someone can say about us, that we're all honest to a fault, I'd make that into a badge and wear it proudly around this or any town." Audrey lets out a large sob and Sal comforts her.

I look out to all the grieving faces. "Mom, I'm ready for you to be buried in the earth like all our brother and sister wolves before us."

It's funny. No one blinks at the wolf bit. There are three possibilities for this, I think. The first is that my prior odd behaviors have made a moment like this typical. My family might just be blowing off this random canus lupus stuff as some writer bullshit.

The second is my family is so damn odd that an oddity like this one doesn't pop out. The third is I didn't even actually utter the last bit because I'm losing the capacity to decipher what is being thought in my wolf brain and what I am speaking aloud in the "regular" world. Number three is the most interesting and terrifying possibility.

Lauren and the family gather post burial. This is a different sort of party than the one for my homecoming a couple of weeks back. Some things are the same. My uncles and Sal are getting drunk on Labatt Blue. We're all eating from a platter of egg salad sandwiches Lauren and Audrey prepared. I have this feeling if Lauren and Audrey weren't here all of us men would never eat again and probably die. That's because men are stupid and weak and women are smart and strong. I suppose I'm pretty intoxicated, too.

Wild Turkey and egg salad go surprisingly well together when you haven't eaten in twenty-four hours. Truth be told, I've been drinking Wild Turkey all day from a flask. It's not that I was trying to be dishonest with you about my earlier drinking, I just didn't think of mentioning it. Even Audrey is drinking a beer. Her somewhat sloppy manner indicates she's a little tipsy. I watch her as she tips her glass back and a heaviness develops in her eyes.

"I need you to help me with something," she says. Lauren looks at me and gives me a little nod.

"Okay."

Audrey gestures and I follow her into the garage. I assume she wants me to restock the cooler with beer or something. But as soon as the door swings shut behind us, Audrey grabs my hand and holds it tight with her old crow claw. "You know I loved your mother, right?"

"Yes. I know."

"And you know I loved your father, too?"

"Yes."

"Your father and I… We made a mistake… a beautiful mistake that came out of love. I never meant to hurt your mother. No one else knows. Only Frank, Camilla, and me. And I'm sorry for what Frank and I did. Your father and I paid for our mistake, as did your dear mom. But Little Sal paid most of all."

Maybe I've been drinking too much the last couple of days but what Audrey is telling me is not computing in my wolf brain, or my man brain.

"I don't understand," I slur.

Little Sal enters the garage and even he knows he's stepped into something big. "I'm just grabbing a beer for Uncle Spider," he says apologetically. When I see Audrey's eyes, everything is clear to me. Sal and I are fucking brothers!

"All good, man," I stammer as I grab a beer from the cooler and chuck it at Sal harder than I intend. He fields it well like when we played Little League together.

"You good, bro?"

It's amazing that I'm able to get the words, "I'm fine," out of my mouth considering how much I'm grinding my teeth.

"You okay, Mom?"

"I'm just sad," Audrey says.

Audrey's right. We are a sad, little family built on top of one colossally huge fucking lie. I thought we were too honest. That was wrong. My mendacity detector is still broken. I've been misguided about so many things.

Sal leaves the garage because he doesn't really want to touch whatever the hell is going on.

"Sal doesn't know," Audrey says.

"Why tell me then?"

"With your mom passing, I've been thinking about what's going to happen to Sal when I go. You're brothers, and you need to know that."

"Then, why don't you tell your son?"

"I love, Sal. But I don't know if he can take the truth. His entire life he's been trying to live up to his father, only he believes his father is the wrong man and I promised Camilla I wouldn't tell him. That was our deal. But Sal needs a brother, now. He needed a brother his whole life. I'm sorry to put all this on you. This isn't how I planned it. This isn't how I planned my life."

Audrey drops into my arms and sobs. I hold her there in the garage in the dark. With my leg, I use the beer cooler to prop both of us up so we won't fall.

I have a brother. I have a drug-dealing brother.

FIFTEEN
WOLF COMES TO PLAY

It's late. Lauren took off to her parents' place to check in on them. I'm discovering this woman is very loyal and different from my ex, who is an assassin in a silk nightie made with a million cheap lies. It warms my heart to imagine my ex on a plane back home. Fear comes over me as I guess the distance between Buffalo and Virginia. What if a new transportation system is created that greatly reduces travel time? I wish Virginia was a place much farther away in a distant country on another planet.

Lauren's instinct isn't to leave. She's just like Camilla, in the fight until it's over. It's a wonderful thing generally, though I now understand why Frank retreated to the bathroom as his office away from work. Sometimes it's hard to be cared for so well and so thoroughly.

The truth is I talked Lauren into going home for the evening. She's been so giving to me and my family that I'm worried about her well-being. Lauren deserves better than to be stuck in some sort of constant nurturing purgatory. I never thought I needed so much, but upon receiving Lauren's care I think I can get used to it.

The other reason I sent Lauren home is I want a chance to talk to Sal alone. Apparently, Sal wants the same thing. He's the last one in the house. Sal's sitting in my writing chair in the dark, looking out the bay window. I sit in the chair beside him where Camilla used to watch me write. The chair feels so familiar I almost forget Mom is no longer here. I flip on the light. As Sal turns toward me I see his face differently. Frank's chiseled chin and his long nose are there. Growing up, I always wanted a brother. At first, I wanted a playmate. Then, when I grew older and began to understand my parents' difficulty at conceiving and the pain and friction that trouble caused, I wanted a sibling for them.

I would have accepted a sister from God, but in my secret prayers I always asked for a brother. Honestly, they weren't so much prayers as they were intense negotiations. Camilla had told me I should never negotiate with God. Of course, that's why I did it every night. I promised God I'd be good if he gave me a brother. Neither party seemed to keep the bargain. I thought I hadn't been good enough. Maybe I was good enough after all. Or maybe I was kind of good just like I'm kind of a man and kind of a wolf, so God kind of gave me a brother. I watch as Sal gulps the rest of his beer too fast, chokes a little, clears his airway by beating on his chest like a cave man, and then cleans off the spilt beer from the shadow of my father's chin.

"We got to talk, man," Sal implores.

"Sure thing, bro," I utter without really meaning to say bro at all.

"You're a smart guy, right?"

"I'm not really smart. I'm more self-aware to a fault."

"Whatever, man. What are you saying?" Sal belches.

"Just that I'm aware of my own bullshit but it hasn't stopped me from running into wall after wall headfirst like my head is a demolition crew."

"You're kinda strange."

"You know what. You're right." I crush my empty beer against my forehead and toss it aside.

"Do you want another beer or something?" Sal asks.

"No, I think we should talk."

"So do I."

I jump right in at the opportunity. "I've learned some things here recently that have been pretty disturbing."

"I know. I know. And I haven't lied, not really. It's just complicated."

"You mean, you know, too?" I probe.

"What are you talking about? Of course I know. I don't want to be dealing drugs."

I'm not really listening here. There's a way to hear but not really listen. I tend to do that when Sal goes on a monologue. He's obviously about to go on one because he's up and pacing as the beer is spilling out of his can with his exaggerated gesticulations.

While I tune him out, Sal continues, "I mean I did want to at first but that was just a little weed here and there. But then the cops got involved. They popped me for weed and Neel for making a pipe bomb that blew up his parents' basement. Neel's a good kid. He wasn't doing it to blow up the school or anything. He just has a scientific mind and building the pipe bomb was something to do like when you and I were his age playing street hockey. The cops latest cook died unexpectedly and they realized Neel could do it for them and I could distribute. I already had all the contacts."

Sal finally sits back down, puts his hands on his knees and leans in for my response. He reminds me of a guy who was taught a constructive listening posture in a counseling class.

"Audrey told me today that you..." I say. Then I focus in on the smashed beer can on the floor. "Wait a second... you're dealing drugs with the Cheektowaga police." I guess I really was listening. My brain records everything in case I need to hear it.

Sal interrupts, "Mom knows?"

"She doesn't know. Let's get back to the fact you and Neel are cooking meth for the cops."

"It's not meth. They're Molly pills. What the hell did Mom tell you today?"

I spit out, "She told me... She told me that you and I are brothers."

The blood drains from Sal's face. "We're brothers, bro? How? What?" Then his eyes brighten. Somewhere in the folds of his brain he's always known. "We're brothers."

I get up. Sal does the same. He holds open his arms like I only wish God would do. They're scrawny and bird-like. He looks weak, but he's not. My father had those arms. I have those arms, too. Our arms can build entire cities or tear them down, depending on where the money is and how we feel about existence. I raise my arms, slow at first, and then wide like a seabird who, having just landed after a long uncertain journey because he's directionally impaired, spreads out his wings to shake off a deep itch.

We meet in the middle of the living room. Our scrawny arms might conjure an image of a seabird, but we're no damn birds. We're wolves in a city of wolves in a world of wolves. Sal and I are two wolf-man pups, almost grown but not quite, who found each other in the night after years of following the fading, haunting echo wolf-call of our father, who howled out his name one last time in the night before he breathed his last. We've finally found our father in each other's eyes. The moon is out. It's nearly full.

A primordial sound crescendos throughout the house; throughout the entire damn town; throughout the whole damned world. Sal and I are both sobbing and howling together.

A spiral of smoke in front of me morphs into a wolf's head. The plume dissipates in the living room between us. Sal passes me a joint and I take a big hit. There're benefits to having a drug dealer for a brother. We're drinking Crown Royal, a Canadian whiskey. It shouldn't be too surprising by now most high-quality Buffalo things are actually Canadian things. I say that not to denigrate Buffalo's standing in the world but to give credit where it's due to our northerly neighbors who still honor the monarchy.

"I got some deep shit to ask you, man," Sal says.

"Go for it."

"Why'd you leave, Tommy?"

"I don't know, Sal. The weather." The whiskey burns my throat. That's what I get for not being completely honest. This place has never felt comfortable for me and it's always been that way. When I was younger, I felt I had to leave because I wanted to be a writer and you couldn't be a writer in Buffalo. I know that's untrue, now. One can be a writer wherever one writes.

Leaving was really about getting away from Camilla and Frank. As a child, I'd look at my parents and wonder if I was an alien. The truth is I felt my parents were holding me back. My parents are gone now, and I am the person I am now for better or worse. The reasons for running away from home are fading, yet the feeling remains like an echo shouted in a cavern behind Niagara Falls. Now, Sal and I can be aliens together. "It was just something I had to do."

"I don't want to deal drugs no more, bro. But they won't let me stop. The cops say they'll kill me, Neel, and Priya," Sal says.

"They won't..."

"You bet your ass they will. You don't know these guys like I do. You want another pill?" Sal's talking about Molly – you know, MDMA. It's not a regular thing for me. Sal claims it helps you feel connected, and I need that tonight. About thirty minutes ago, we took a couple of pills. At least, I think it was only two pills.

Out of his pocket, Sal procures a handful of tablets. "Take another," he says.

"Is that safe?"

"Yeah, man."

I take it because fuck it.

"What should I do?" Sal asks.

"I don't know."

"Then I'm fucked. I've got no one else."

There's one idea, but should I say it? Fuck it. He's my bro and he needs me. Maybe it's the MDMA but he'll accept it, however crazy it seems. He loves me and I love him, too. "There's this turkey in the field I've been talking to," I spit out.

"Gobble, gobble?" Sal asks.

"More or less. But he, like, talks and stuff. I know it's nuts but he gives me advice. His name is Oliver. We can, like, journey into the field and find him."

"This is a great idea, Tommy."

Clinking glasses, we toast our forthcoming journey.

Sal and I stumble toward the woods. This is the best idea I've ever had and I am fantastic. My brain is addled but in a good and liberated way. Irrational times call for irrational measures. The rational world put us into trouble in the first place so the irrational world will get us out. Also, the War on Drugs, a corrupt Cheektowaga Police Department, and at least one carnal act between our parents many years prior put us in this mess. Sal strips off his shirt. "What are you doing?" I ask.

"The air is cool. It's also easier to battle bugs that attack you if you can see them on your skin."

"Good idea." I take off my shirt, too.

Sal carries a mop bucket. I think we intend to carry Oliver back in the bucket. He also has a broom. I have a toilet brush I'm wearing like a sword in one of my father's old belts. The brush is mostly clean of crap. We're both wearing a couple of our father's fedoras, for obvious reasons. Why am I wearing the toilet sword? Oh, yes, I remember. It's becoming clearer, foggier, clearer. This toilet brush is to throttle Oliver with if he gives us any shit.

We are deep in the woods. "Oliver! Oliver!" I scream out, my voice cracking from the chill and cotton mouth from all the dope I smoked. Sal and I didn't bring any beer to drink to satiate our thirst. You can't think of everything.

Sal picks up where I left off, "Oliver, Oliver!"

"Shhh, you'll scare Oliver off. He doesn't know your voice," I whisper.

"Sorry."

The moon is two-thirds full. Between my third of a brain and Sal's slightly less than a third we are still over one third short of a brain.

Sal and I both hear claws scraping together in the dark. We huddle close, back-to-back. Sal's broom is at the ready as is my toilet brush.

Oliver descends on us with a fierce gobble war cry. Wings are everywhere as Oliver attacks. Sal and I swing wildly. I accidentally jam the toilet brush in Sal's nose; he stabs me with the broom in my testicles.

"Please, Oliver," I cry. "It's only me and my cousin/brother, Sal!" The battle comes to a sudden halt and Oliver perches on a nearby branch.

"Sorry, bros. I didn't know it was you. You never can be too careful when you hear people screaming your name in the night. It could be vagabond pirate killers or the voice of God among other frightening things. In any case, I've learned through experience it's better to come down raining claws and apologize later if you've pummeled a friend rather than a foe."

We cower beneath Oliver who no longer appears to me as I

remember him. His eyes are larger and there are actual flames inside them. He is more God than turkey.

"Please, Oliver. Can you tell us what to do? The cops are going to kill Sal and Priya and Neel if he doesn't keep selling their drugs."

Oliver puts his foot in his mouth and picks out a piece of something – likely a piece of my leathery hide from when he pecked my ass in the fray.

In a booming voice Oliver calls out, "In the incomparable poetic words from N.W.A., 'Fuck the police'."

I wake up in the woods. Someone is holding me. It's a man. Holy Mother of God, it's a shirtless man. I extricate myself from his clutches and shoot up to my feet. It's only then I realize the man is Sal. He wakes up and looks at me squinting as the rising morning sun shines directly in his eyes between a break in the foliage above.

"What am I supposed to do about the cops, Tommy?" Sal asks.

I look Sal right in his eyes and squint like Clint Eastwood does in all his movies. "Call their damned bluff."

"They'll kill me, man."

"They won't. These are Cheektowaga cops. They might be corrupt assholes but they're not killer assholes. These guys are the football players in high school who built their entire identities on playing a sport they were not good at. Their power complex is founded upon the premise they will not be challenged for their baseless ass-hattery. I remember back in high school the jocks were picking on this skater kid in the parking lot and he stood up to them and then the jocks didn't even know what to do, so they left him alone."

"So, we're the football players in this story?"

"We're the skater kid, Sal. If you stand up to these cops, they'll move on. They're not brave enough or smart enough to do anything else."

Back at the house, I hold Sal's hand as he calls his contact at the Cheektowaga police. Tears well in his eyes as his voice quivers into the phone. "I can't do it no more, Pete."

Pete Karkowski's in on this, too! I knew I shouldn't have trusted that son of a bitch.

"We're out," Sal squeaks like a tiny mouse caught in a trap. "Please don't be mad. I'm trying to make some changes. It isn't you or the guys, it's me. I just don't feel like I can be the man I want to be and keep doing this, Pete."

Sal turns to me. "He hung up. What do you think that means?"

I'm not going to tell Sal this call reminds me of the breakup conversation I had with my ex. The breakup didn't go smoothly thereafter. I figure I don't need to scare him. To my great surprise given the cynical self-story I've created over the years, I've also realized I'm actually an optimist.

"I think I should talk to Neel and get rid of the stuff," Sal says. "There's no telling what the cops will do. They might try to pin all this shit on us. Will you go over to Neel's and help me?"

"I don't think that's a great idea. I don't want Priya to get the wrong idea boundary-wise."

"What do you mean?" Sal asks.

"It's a long story."

"Tell me."

"She presented herself to me."

"What do you mean? Like she gave you a present or something?"

"She presented herself... naked."

"I see. I was not aware of that, Tommy. That is awkward. You didn't fuck her, did you?"

"Of course not."

"Then you're good." Sal grins as he smacks me on the shoulder.

I guess it's as simple as Sal makes it. Simplicity can be very freeing. I am good, and I didn't do anything wrong.

"Fine. I'll help."

———

Neel takes exiting from the drug business in stride and Priya isn't home, thankfully. He wants out, too. Neel only wants to go to the University of Buffalo to become an engineer and get girls. He never wanted to cook drugs. Neel never wanted any of this. We don't ask to be born into a world of corruption. No one asks to be born at all. But here we are and all most of us want to do is make the best of it and get girls or whatever we're into.

The three of us – Neel, Sal, and I – are in the woods, right near the dead end. Sal drove his truck a bit off-road up the path as far as he could go. Crabapple Court is partially visible through the trees from our position and we're hoping no one can see us from their homes. We're emptying Sal's truck of all the chemicals and tools Neel used to cook the pills. It's gray out and getting darker as the day becomes evening. The neighborhood is dead quiet, except for a faulty electric street lamp nearby that buzzes and then stops.

There's a hockey stick in the truck partly buried under a tarp. Wait a second. It's my hockey stick! The one I told you about. It's the hockey stick I had signed by Richard Smehlik after the "Shoot, Pass, and Skate Competition." It was gone forever, I thought, like so many lost artifacts of youth, but here it is in Sal's truck.

I drop the blue barrel I'm helping Sal unload and pick up the hockey stick like Arthur plucking out Excalibur. "You stole my hockey stick!"

"I didn't," Sal says. "You gave it to me after my father died. Don't you remember?"

I don't remember. "Why do you have it in here?"

"Cooking takes a long time and Neel wants to learn how to play hockey so he doesn't get his ass kicked in gym class anymore. I've been showing him some moves because I got mad skills. Neel's getting pretty good. Believe it or not, the kid's got a hell of a cross check."

Neel beams then gets a little shy as he lowers his head.

"You use an autographed Richard Smehlik stick to play street hockey?" I ask as the incredulity rises in my voice.

"After all this shit that we've done and we're doing right now, that's the thing you're gonna take issue with?"

Sal has a point. Using the autographed stick to play hockey is not our biggest problem right now. Still, using the stick for playing street hockey seems wrong. Smehlik wasn't the best Sabres player but he was a solid defenseman. His autograph deserves respect. Smehlik was steady. That's what we need to see us through this ordeal, steadiness.

"Fuck!" Sal shouts as the barrel slips through his hands and thuds on the ground.

"Be quiet. Let's hurry up and get this done."

As Sal and I return to unloading the barrel, I can't help but think about the hockey stick. We can think something is lost, like an autographed hockey stick or the neurotic fear our childhood innocence is missing, and then after so many years it's still there, right under our noses. In fact, it's been there the entire time, waiting for me, safeguarded by the other that is my brother, but I had forgotten I gave it to him for safekeeping.

———

Neel and Sal are playing a hockey video game. I'm cradling the hockey stick and staring at Smehlik's faded autograph. Only a few letters remain. Isn't that fitting? There're always letters missing from the words we've written on our hearts, and all we can do is attempt to fill in the empty spaces and try to resurrect those old words so they can make meaning again.

Priya enters through the front door. She's modestly dressed and wearing a long sweater. Maybe this means she's taking all I said to heart. I guess I shouldn't be focused on how she's dressed. It seems too close to focusing on other corporeal things I will not do. It's best not to allow thoughts to grow that ought not. Priya leans her backside against the kitchen counter.

"Would you like to stay for dinner?" she asks.

Sal immediately says yes as I spit out, "No, thank you."

"I'm making paneer," Priya offers.

"You got to stay, bro. Her paneer is amazing. It's cheese, bro."

"No, really. I can't. But thank you for the offer." I shake Neel's hand and then ask Sal about the stick. "Can I borrow this back?"

"Sure. Why?"

"I don't know. Maybe I'll practice my wrist shot later."

"Yeah, okay, Tommy. I'll stop by after dinner."

I look back at Priya and she seems okay, really okay. Maybe she's figuring everything out and that's all we can hope for each other. Priya adjusts position again and every move is like a pose. She'd be a great Parisian. Priya has that awareness of watching and being watched Parisian women all have. This latest pose reminds me a little of Venus de Milo. Except, of course, Priya has both her arms attached to her body and she's fully clothed in reality, and in my mind and, for that, I am very grateful.

I nod to Neel and then Priya and take my leave.

Writing has been impossible since Camilla died. I haven't even pretended to write. But now I find myself sitting in my chair in the living room as before. In my imagination, Camilla is seated in hers across from me. Sometimes she's looking out the bay window. On occasion she glances at me and reads my face to try to figure out what I'm writing. She hopes I'm writing about her. I can't blame her really. If I ever have kids and they become writers, I'll want them to write about me, too. I hope they don't just write about all the ways I've failed them. It'd be ideal if they write about my great effort to do otherwise with an occasional smirk of gratefulness.

Of course, Camilla was totally right. Everything is about her. All my writing has always been about her. And that's true for any of us. Our parents have that sort of stranglehold on us. We think we're living for ourselves, but it's always for them. Their blood calls out to our blood and makes each of our movements not quite our own. And then it's our duty to do the same thing to our kids. We have to give our messiest, most beautiful selves to our children so they will continue on and do the same to their own children so all of us can live forever.

I look up from my mad writing to see the Buffalo News van with the Cheektowaga Police Department bumper sticker speed up the street and park in Priya and Neel's driveway. Four plainclothes cops, including that corrupt asshole Pete Karkowski, hop out and head to the front door. At least two of them are poorly concealing shotguns in their Buffalo Bills winter jackets. I may have underestimated their resolve.

My cell phone rings. It's Lauren. On autopilot, I pick up. "Hi Lauren."

"Hi Tommy. We need to talk. It's important."

I drop the phone to the ground. Something has come over me. I am of no mind. All action. Total instinct. I animal.

Grabbing the hockey stick, I hop over the coffee table, and sprint out the front door.

Outside Priya and Neel's front door, I hear cheers, a crash, a shriek, laughter, and then another shrill scream. Kicking open the door, I see Sal, Priya, and Neel tied to kitchen chairs in the living room. Pete and his three cop buddies are standing behind them. No one notices me. Two police are playing the NHL video game on the big screen with the volume turned up extremely loud. The third has his shotgun drawn at Sal. When the audience on the game cheers, Pete smacks Sal in the back of the head. I step inside. This is the abusive game they've been playing. What a bunch of pricks. Corrupt motherfuckers. The other cops laugh at Neel's squeal, and Priya screams again.

Do something. "Fuck you, Pete! You always sucked at football in high school, and your girlfriend was super into me!" I yell.

The officer with the shotgun trains it on me. "What are you going to do with that stick, asshole? Put it down."

Pete spins toward me. "Shut the door, Tommy." I lower the hockey stick. Sal and Neel seem exhausted, defeated.

"This is how you choose to live your life? You fraud," I say.

"Look at yourself, Tommy. Like you're some big-time success. You're a divorced loser, pining over a teenage girl." Pete touches Priya's cheek and she recoils. "She's not so innocent. We all know that." The other officers laugh.

"Leave her alone, Pete. She's a kid."

"I've done my research on you, pal," Pete retorts.

"This can't be about the money. There's got to be better ways."

Pete steps toward me. "Like moving to Los Angeles, failing at everything you do, and pretending to be somebody. You're nobody, Tommy. And you've got nothing. You're unemployed. You have no money. Your mom's dead. There's no reason for you to even be here anymore. You're not one of us. I always knew you weren't right in high school. You're a goddamned freak! I can't wait until Lauren pieces it all together!"

I am blind rage. The only thing I feel is the weight of the hockey stick balanced in my hands. My mind clicks to black.

The blackness lifts slowly like walking away from a mist in the evening toward a distant light. When I come back to consciousness, the first thing I see is Priya staring blankly at me. Her whole body shakes. Priya's terrified of me. Neel and Sal have that same look; one of bewilderment and fear. There's blood everywhere; even on my hands, splattered all over the walls. All around the room are shotgun blasts; some in the walls and others though the sofas and into the kitchen. There's an older Indian woman here.

"My God, my God, my God!" she screams. An Indian man is here, too. His hands are on his head, like he's trying to hold his brain from seeping out. These must be Priya and Neel's parents. What the hell did I do to cause these reactions?

The hockey stick is no longer in my hands. The butt of it is sticking in Pete's asshole. He is slumped over on the floor. Pete looks like a broken puppet and might be dead. All the shady cops appear lifeless.

Lauren's in front of me suddenly. "What did you do Tommy?" She draws her hand over her mouth at the horror of the scene.

"I don't know. How did you get here?" I ask.

"I was concerned about you." Lauren takes a deep breath and then lets it all out. "I'm pregnant!" She places her hand over her belly.

This is not computing. "Pardon me?"

"There's a baby inside me!" she reiterates.

"Congratulations," Sal says. He pats me on the back.

Perplexed, I cock my head.

Lauren turns to Sal. "What did Tommy do?"

"It's a little hard to explain," Sal evades.

Lauren grabs Sal by the shirt collar. "I don't give a shit if it's difficult. You tell me what the hell is going on. And you do it fast."

"Tommy saved us," Sal squawks.

"He did? But why?" Lauren asks.

Sal gestures at the police like he's a waiter guiding a family toward their table. "I got into some trouble with these guys. They're crooked Cheektowaga police. It was over drugs I was selling for them, but I wanted to stop and they wouldn't let me. So, they tied us all up and threatened to hurt Neel and Priya if I didn't get back with the program."

"That's terrible," Lauren says.

Sal senses Lauren is coming over to his side. "Tommy's a hero. They were going to kill us. Tommy swung his stick like a martial artist or something and whacked the biggest one of them upside the head. The cop fell down while firing a blast from his shotgun. All the other cops fired their guns, too. Bullets were flying all over. It's a miracle none of us were hit. Tommy moved faster than I've ever seen anybody before. At some point, he was scampering on all fours and bounding from one cop to the next. I swear there were fangs coming out of his mouth. Tommy bit one of the other guys on the shoulder and then threw him against the wall. This knocked him straight out."

Lauren gawks at me as if I have a new misshapen appendage attached to my forehead, and then gapes at the unfortunately placed hockey stick stuck in an unlucky bottom nearby. "What happened to this guy? Wait a sec… is that Pete?

"Yes, it's him," I inform.

"Pete was the last one standing. He raised his Glock to shoot Tommy. From all fours, Tommy jumped through the air and head-butted Pete. The hockey stick landed funny against the coffee table in the melee and broke in half. Somehow when Pete was falling to the ground unconscious, the butt of the stick went straight up his ass."

"I can see that, Sal," Lauren says.

Cutting through the cacophony of the video game and occasional screams from Priya's mother is the clear sound of sirens approaching.

Lauren takes out her cell. I'm calling my cousin. He's an FBI agent. He'll know what to do.

Crossing my legs, I sit on the floor and practice deep breathing I learned in a yoga class.

Lauren having a cousin in the Bureau, and placed locally at that, may seem coincidental, but you should be getting used to it by now – everything is connected in this town. Her cousin Sam is a good guy, a little uptight with clenched ass cheeks at times, but a good man when it comes down to what's important – a sense of family responsibility. I got off pretty easy.

It turns out the Cheektowaga cops in question had long been suspected of corruption. The local authorities had been inclined to cover for their own, so I actually did the entire community a service by shedding light on their criminal activities. It helped my conscience, and the story sold to the people of Buffalo through The Buffalo News, that I didn't actually kill any of the cops. All of them were mostly fine, with only cosmetic damage that will fade over time. Even Pete's butthole will be okay after a period of convalescence.

I almost feel sorry for Pete. Sometimes I wonder if I could have faced the downward trajectory of his life if I had never left Cheektowaga. It's not impossible to fathom. Maybe, like him, my world would have become small with past minor successes in high school the only thing to bring to the altar of life's meaning. Perhaps those trivial accomplishments would have burned too quickly, and then I might have focused on reclaiming the power I'd lost in pursuit of money as power.

But then I think about my time in Hollywood. I never quite fit in that small world in the same way I never fit in the small world of Cheektowaga. And that's not to say I think of myself as too big or smart or anything. It's just the way it is… it's a feeling of never belonging in small spaces. I owe that feeling to Frank and Camilla. They had this way of making me feel big and undercutting me at the same time. It helped me develop an ego big enough to avoid small-mindedness but small enough not to become an egomaniacal asshole.

SIXTEEN

WOLF PACK

Lauren requested a second talk about the pregnancy. My mind wasn't right for the first chat, and it didn't go particularly well. At the time, we had more pressing matters. Looking out the window at the bare crabapple tree, I can't help but feel there is some latent energy inside it that is about to burst forth in a stupendous act of creation. You know by now I do have an overactive imagination. Sometimes a bare tree is just a bare tree. Maybe that's my koan and I need to learn to accept that. I watch as Lauren pulls up in her old Escort.

She steps out of her car and walks up to my door. Her gait has this stiff quality she sometimes has when she's stressed out. I read her stress and incorporate it into my body. My back is suddenly aching and, God, I feel old. A million years have passed by the last several weeks. I'm too old to be a father to anybody. Taking care of myself is precarious enough already. And what if the wolf comes out again? I can't be trusted. It's well established I'm a danger to myself and to others. I cannot and will not be a father.

The doorbell rings four times as I pace back and forth. On the fifth ring, I swing the door wide open. Lauren has something in her eyes. It's not fear. It's not sadness. It's love. She has love in her eyes, and the feeling I have for her and our baby is multiplied in my countenance and returned back to her. The tensions in both of our bodies diminish and she doesn't need to say a word. I take her hand and guide her into the living room and I have this sense Camilla is in her chair watching over us. Holding Lauren in my arms, I suddenly feel strong like one of those huge body builders in Venice, California. We kiss and she cries and I cry, too.

Lauren says, "I'm a little scared."

"Me too, but everything is going to be okay and I'm going to be here for all of us, always. I promise you that." I look out over her shoulder and see the crabapple tree. The goddamn thing is blooming the most beautiful white flowers. And this wave comes over me like I'm in the ocean and I'm knocked under the water but then it passes and I get up and can breathe. I can finally breathe.

My whole life I was running from Cheektowaga, from Buffalo, from my parents and myself. I used to have the worst irrational fears about impregnating someone from my hometown and then having to stay here the rest of my life. Well, that's happened, and I am terrified. But I'm afraid and excited, too, because I love Lauren and this baby can be the best thing we've ever created.

Frank was a flawed man. He slept with his cousin's wife and had my half-brother Sal, who he never claimed as his own. My father took his secret to the grave. But I believe he loved all of us, including Audrey and Sal. Dad did wrong but he was not proud of it. And he never acted like Sal was wrong. Frank went out of his way to include Sal in the family in the manner he thought he could. I think he could have done much more.

Camilla kept my father's secret, too. She held a grudge against Audrey, but only so far. Both my parents were flawed and so am I, but in my family there was always love, and that's what I can wholeheartedly promise to provide. I can promise I will try to do what's right for my family. If I do wrong, I will not be proud of it. Being honest and correcting my shortcomings will be a daily practice. Lauren touches my face and I place my hand on her stomach.

Little baby, I promise you I will do my best to guide you through this beautiful mess of a world.

―――――――

Life is a wondrous calamity. It's always messing about your face. Sometimes it bites and tears. Other times it kisses and coos. Often it bites while kissing. I can't say any of this is particularly surprising once there is acceptance of what an utterly absurd cup life is; filled to the brim with forthright meaning sloshing around in a mess of brine water; often spilling over the sides from reality to dreams.

My consistency has changed. I don't feel like an undead/wolf man as much anymore. The wolf really came out to play. His violence was necessary but it frightens me. We want to know we have the capacity to protect those we love. But now I know it, I'll happily let the wolf rest. Deep down I feel he's there inside me; waiting and ready should the need arise for a resurrection. Oliver doesn't come to me in the fields much anymore either, and my trips there have wound down, too. I suppose I needed Oliver and the wolf in my conscious life awhile but now they can take a sabbatical and come to me solely in my dreams from time to time.

Sleep has been coming more easily lately. For a long time, I never thought that would happen. I sleep at least eight solid hours each night. My dreams are a little dark still, but sweet, too, in a way I prefer. Camilla comes to me in my dreams, and Frank, too. I dream of the smell of Mom's awful cooking, and the way she'd laugh at her own jokes. Her eyes still smile when she knows I know exactly what she's thinking. I dream of my father's calloused hand gently brushing my face. And I dream of Dad yelling out behind the restroom door, demanding some peace and quiet.

My ex-wife, Barbara, appears less and less in my dreams. Before, I thought if I whispered her name she'd show up like a great demon to terrorize me. I can say her name now because she holds so much less power. Barbara, I forgive you. Also, fuck you, Barbara.

Camilla, Frank, Oliver, and the wolf are all kind of like my dead family now. As family, they hassle me a little in my dreams. But not like Barbara and the terrors she inspired. It's the right sort of bother. It's that familial ghost tickle that hits a nerve in the right way.

Sometimes I dream about Priya, too. Mostly I have dreams about her long dark hair. It always covers her entire body. I honestly don't think it's sexual, but a matter of appreciation. Priya reminds me that, in some ways, we are all innocent and confused and just need people to guide us on our way without taking advantage of the fact we are works in progress.

I had complicated feelings about Priya and that's okay. Feelings aren't actions and neurotic guilt over passing primal thoughts is not the same thing as acting them out and causing another's pain. We should let ourselves off the hook for the wild animal thoughts we never act on. Beating ourselves up only gives us bruises; it doesn't turn us into angels.

Pride follows close behind growth, but it comes with a new humility, too. People never seem to fit inside boxes. Why the hell should they anyway? Maybe I'm growing up. I've learned it's important to feel good about oneself. It helps to look inside and be able to say, "Hey, guy. You're okay. You might have your flaws, but you see them, face them, and try not to hurt anybody including yourself. Dammit, you're really okay."

Lauren's never in my dreams, and that doesn't worry me. I never dream about her because we exist in the real world. When I wake up, she's by my side and we are together in this journey. Sometimes

I fall asleep on her stomach listening to the blossoming poems of our baby/cub. Other times I wake up and we're holding hands. This does not freak me out one bit. It's vulnerability. Intimacy may be new territory but it's the terrain I've wanted to explore my entire life. I tell you what, it's nice to feel truly safe with someone.

When I awake after a long sleep, drunk on the never-ending cup of my darkly-sweet dreams, I don't have any anxiety about writing. I don't care if it will come again or if that cup has run out. It never really runs out. People matter. Family is important. If my writing conveys that, then maybe it'll be meaningful, too.

I started out wanting to write a novel about a man who feared he was becoming a wolf. That book remains unfinished because I became that wolf man for a little while. Instead, I ended up writing a novel about the time I returned home to help my mother die. It's about how she taught me to die and to live; how I came to better understand my dead father, reconnected with my cousin who is really my brother, and learned the truth doesn't have to set you free. Instead, it can bind you ever tighter to your imperfect family and that's okay, too.

Life is a funny cup. It's a funny, overflowing, cracked cup teetering and spinning on a narrow, taut rope across a great divide. One moment I am asleep in my childhood bed drunk on my dreams and the next the whole world is shaking. Cheektowaga is on a fault line. It's not just the fault line between the middle class and the poor. It's not just the fault between good and evil or the fault line between reality and dreams. Cheektowaga sits on an actual fault line. Actually, hundreds of crisscrossed fault lines run under the ground. People used to think the Appalachian Plateau under the earth was pretty tame. They were mistaken.

The big one was coming. I could feel it in my bones. But how could I know it was going to be in Cheektowaga? The quake was a 5.5 on the Richter scale and Cheektowaga was the epicenter. In fact, the epicenter was on my very block right in front of Camilla's house. No one was hurt and there was no major structural damage. A few wall hangings crashed to the floor. The crucifix didn't move an inch. Upon seeing it still in its place and the clock next to it shattered on the floor, I imagined Camilla's ghost there, holding onto both of them. I pictured the shaking was too much so she let the clock go and held onto her savior. Her decision made sense to me. We ought to hold onto what's most important to us and let the rest go. Later, I thought better about where Camilla really was when the earthquake happened. She wasn't in the kitchen at all. Lauren and I had fallen asleep in the living room. Mom was standing protectively over us, holding our heads in her big hands, like those of a loving God, there to keep us from any harm.

ABOUT KEVIN DEL PRINCIPE

Kevin Del Principe is a writer and film director. The son of a snowplow truck driver and a school nurse, Kevin grew up outside of Buffalo, New York. He now lives in Los Angeles and teaches screenwriting at Loyola Marymount University. Kevin directed and co-wrote the feature film, UP ON THE GLASS and earned his MFA in Writing for Screen and Television at the USC School of Cinematic Arts.

www.kevindelprincipe.com

OTHER BOOKS FROM TUMBLEWEED

You may also enjoy the following books published by Tumbleweed Books

All the Devils are Here by Michael Saad

The Steam Room Diaries by Cameron Miller

Realizing River City by Melissa Grunow

Memories of Korea by Seong-min Yoo

Bear's Dancing Shoes by Seong-min Yoo